THE LONELY TIGER

THE LONELY TIGER

HUGH ALLEN

RAINLIGHT
RUPA

Published in Rainlight by
Rupa Publications India Pvt. Ltd 2014
7/16, Ansari Road, Daryaganj
New Delhi 110002

Sales centres:
Allahabad Bengaluru Chennai
Hyderabad Jaipur Kathmandu
Kolkata Mumbai

ISBN: 978-81-291-3125-6

First impression 2014
10 9 8 7 6 5 4 3 2 1

Typeset by Jojy Philip, New Delhi

Printed at Replika Press Pvt Ltd., India

CONTENTS

FOREWORD

BRIGHTNESS AND TERROR IN THE JUNGLE

As a boy, much before I devoured Jim Corbett, I happened upon a book called *The Lonely Tiger* by Hugh Allen in my father's bookshelf. I read it with unwavering ferocity, so brilliantly was it written, and as with things that leave their mark it has stayed with me ever since.

Last week, I picked it up and re-read it with the sort of delight that enveloped me the first time I chanced upon the book. For Allen, who died in 1968, is the sort of writer who brings to his hunting stories the pacing and ability to build narrative tension that only the best thriller writers are able to manage. Add to this an encyclopaedic knowledge of the jungle and the animals he hunts and it's easy to see why he belongs to the very select band of shikar writers who are acknowledged masters of the genre—Corbett, Patterson and quite frankly I cannot think of a third.

To the best of my knowledge, this is Allen's only book. He wrote for magazines and the occasional newspaper but *The Lonely Tiger* was the only book of his that saw print. All of the stories that feature in it took place in or around Mandikhera, the estate in the middle of the Madhya Pradesh jungles that Allen bought soon after he was discharged from hospital (he was wounded in the Second World War).

One of the few Englishmen to remain in India after Independence, he farmed his estate with his widowed sister Babs. In between his duties on the farm, he went after wounded tigers and leopards that preyed on livestock, boars that ate up the crop, and other jungle dwellers that every now and again turned rogue. It was a life he thoroughly enjoyed. In an epilogue to the book, he writes: 'Has it all been worth it? And do we ever regret choosing to live in a lonely place like this?

'As I write these words more than ten years have passed and that is time enough to have made up our minds one way or the other. The truth is that we would not change this life for any other, and it would also be true to say that we hardly miss the old kind of life at all.

'Many of our old friends have admitted that since the war they have found it hard to settle down to the old routine and that there are often times when they are bored to tears.

'This, I think, would eventually have happened to me. That it has not and that I am never bored is almost certainly because anything that happens here is real and life is often full of surprises.'

It is the 'surprises' that make up the meat of the book—a badmash leopard, a wounded tiger, a vicious old boar, a deadly Russell's viper.

Each of these adventures is narrated with economy, precision, astonishing atmospherics—and in prose that can only be described as polished and shining. The reader can hear the spine-chilling 'aouff' of a wounded tiger and the alarmed 'wow-ou, wow-ou' belling of sambhar hinds, the chattering monkeys that have glimpsed a concealed leopard and the snorting of an enraged she-bear.

Despite the fact that this was first published as a shikar book, Allen was at heart a conservationist as he writes in his preface. Here the reader will find one of the earliest appeals for the protection of India's endangered wildlife.

Writes the author: 'Half the stories in this book are about animals which have been wounded and not followed up. This is a state of affairs rapidly going from bad to worse. There is now little or no check on illegal shooting. Indeed, the present position is so appalling and the slaughter so great that in a very few years, unless something drastic is done quickly, India will have lost forever much of her finest fauna. That I know has been said many times before and as yet no animal has actually become extinct; just why it is likely to come true this time, and perhaps very soon, will be found in the chapter on the "Lonely Tiger".'

Although it is over fifty years since this book was first published and you would expect that it would date as a lot of non-fiction books do, *The Lonely Tiger* still remains as fresh and spine-tingling and thrilling as it was when I first read it. Sure, we no longer use annas and pice, the jungles that Allen describes have been cut down indiscriminately, and tigers are barely clinging on in the wild, but as with all great books, this one too transcends time, place and quotidian detail to join that select company of true life adventure classics that will last from age to age. This shouldn't come as any real surprise because *The Lonely Tiger* is quite simply the best book that I've ever read on tigers and shikar in India.

David Davidar
January 2014
New Delhi

PREFACE

'For heaven's sake get out while you can!'

That was the advice from nearly all our friends when we told them about Mandikhera. To most of them I suppose it did seem odd to find us negotiating for a large estate in India when the rest of our countrymen were hurrying away from what they believed was suddenly a most uncertain continent. 'You'll never have a moment's peace,' a lot of them warned. 'These Congress chaps are as anti-British as hell. Nearly all of them have been in jail and they're just waiting to pay some of that score back.'

Nothing we heard about the future from any of these friends was ever cheerful, but even when the last of them had left we had not changed our minds. In a short time the sale was through and Mandikhera was ours. It was just what we wanted: a quiet place off the beaten track with enough interest to help us forget the war and how it had unsettled our lives. However, to say that we had chosen it after careful consideration would not have been true. It was one of those things that just happen and we had undoubtedly taken the line of least resistance: we were already in India and fate had already shown us the sort of place we wanted to live in. Indeed, to take the truth a little further, it would be right to say that

Mandikhera was something of a port in a storm, and when we came to it first each of us secretly believed that whatever might happen in the future—either in India or elsewhere—could not matter very much.

That attitude had come about because both of us thought then that our lives had been completely ruined. Babs, who had lived in India before the war, had lost her husband in Malaya and was left with the unattractive prospect of returning to an empty home in England. For more than a year she had lived in a Bombay hotel trying to make up her mind about the future; and it was while she was still wondering what to do that I returned to India and went to see her. Now it was that fate made the first move, for it had been no part of my original plan to see her then but on my way home; and it had also not occurred to me that she would find me a very different brother from the one she had known before the war. I learned the next day what a shock I had been when she remarked that she was surprised to find that I had been allowed to come out alone. I asked her why—and with true sisterly directness she told me: 'Because you're more of a half-wit than I realized and someone ought to be looking after you.'

That was pretty much the truth, and it had come about from a head injury which had left my mind nearly blank for the best part of a year. Then, when things started to return, two complications came with them: like the old professor I was extremely absent-minded while my memory itself was not much better than that of a rather inattentive child. Back at home these two things together had left behind me a trail of open mouths and raised eyebrows. The daily 8.5 to Waterloo was out of the question. I just wasn't prepared to take the risk of what might and could happen to a well-organized office if I were part of it.

I suppose I ran away, not only from that but from a lot of other things as well. I like to think, though, that the doctor sent me when he suggested that a long sea voyage would put everything right. India drew me back like a magnet. It was there I had been in hospital and it was the country I still remembered best. Soon after the ship docked I hauled Babs off to my original objective: the jungles through which I had hunted during wartime leaves. Once in their fastness, I breathed a sigh of relief. Here any little oddities of dress and behaviour would not matter at all, for most sahibs were crazy anyway and scarcely more predictable than the mad dogs about the village.

One day while wandering through the jungles, I came upon the estate of Mandikhera with its four villages nestling in their clearings among the trees. A chance word told me that the owner was selling. We looked the estate over, and although the home farm with its extensive orchards had been neglected for more than fifteen years, we decided that the place was really worth considering. Here was the answer, at least to my own troubles. A quiet life, room to roam with a gun, the only neighbours the simple people of the forest. It intrigued Babs, too for she loves wild places and will keep as many animals as she has the room for. Indeed, before we left from that first inspection, she was already planning what could be done to the house.

As soon as the sale was through, we moved in and started to settle down. The estate certainly was peaceful and we were very much on our own; the only neighbours were the people of the forest and the nearest town for shopping and a few amusements was hundreds of miles away. However, when we had been in some time, several of the big landowners near about started to call on us. Quite naturally they were curious to see what we were like and to find out why we had stayed when the rest of our people had left India. Now an Indian, when he meets you for the first time, is very likely to ply you with questions of a highly personal and intimate kind. But if he asks you what your income is, how many times you have been married and why you did this and not that, he is not being rude but polite by showing a keen interest in your affairs.

On one or two occasions, we told the truth about why we had come to Mandikhera. This, however, opened up such a vast field for further questions that there was just no knowing what was coming next. In the end, I got out a stock answer which was simply: 'I'm very keen on shikar, you know, and my sister likes looking after the ones I don't shoot.' It was part of the truth anyway; for ever since I was old enough to draw back the elastic of a catapult, to hunt big game had been a burning ambition. From a very early age, I had been reading every book about shikar I could get my hands on. When I found Mandikhera I was still reading them and there is little doubt that the thought of all the shooting I should get here influenced my own decision about the estate perhaps more than anything else.

The thought of that now makes me smile when I see how my cherished ambition has actually worked out. All my life I had dreamed of hunting big game and yearned for the opportunity to do it. Yet, when the chance came, I knew almost at once that I was not a true hunter at heart, and I found in practice that I should probably never make a good one. What few successes there have been amount to nothing when ranked beside the failures.

To start with I did a great deal of hunting and killed a large number of animals just for the sport of it. Then all at once, and for a reason that was not immediately clear, I was suddenly less keen. I began to wonder why. The urge to go hunting was still as strong as ever, and whenever I was out the old thrill of stalking an animal was just as fierce. Yet something now was different, though just what it was still escaped me. I went on wondering until one day I realized that the thrill of hunting vanished the second after I had pulled a trigger.

At last, I knew the truth. Two forces were pulling me in different directions. On one side was a real love for all animals, on the other side was that old urge to hunt them. Almost from that moment I laid aside the rifle and took to watching animals instead of shooting them. But if I had been a bad hunter before I was a worse one now for this kind of hunting calls for much more skill if you really want to satisfy your curiosity.

However, I did not give up the rifle entirely for I still hunt for meat and still go after any animal which is better dead. Yet the urge always to hunt with a rifle even after more than ten years in the jungle is as strong as ever; the only difference is that now I know the truth and that the thrill will die the moment I pull the trigger. After that, when I look down on a lifeless body, there comes a pang of remorse and the guilty thought that *there but for me goes a magnificent animal.*

Those last few lines may seem a bit out of place in the preface to a book on shikar. They certainly would be were it not for the fact that there is another side to the penny, and if you live in the jungle and plant crops and keep cattle it's a side that turns up again and again. Indeed, soon after we had planted our first crops I soon found that shooting, whether I liked it or not, was going to form a very definite 'part o'me dooties'.

The land had been ploughed and the seeds sown. The crop was peanuts, and in addition to the old fields we had planted large areas just cleared from the jungle. That year the rains were good. In that rich virgin soil, the plants seemed to spring from the ground while we watched. It was going to be such a bumper crop that we began to wonder what other people found so difficult about farming; and just to show how good we really were, more land was hurriedly ploughed up and put down to the oil seed we call *tili.* These came on fine, too; all we needed now was patience until harvest.

The first marauders from the dark and dripping forests were the fierce wild boars and their sows. As the peanuts started to ripen they were ripping up the fields every night; then the samburs and the mighty blue bulls found the *tili.* A dozen nightwatchmen, sitting on platforms above the field, did little more than keep the damage away from their immediate vicinity.

The nights now were filled with alarms—the belling of frightened sambur hinds; the *WOW-ou! WOW-ou!* of the dainty spotted deer; the sudden galloping stampede of scared pigs. But the jungle was not warning of the men perched above the fields: far more dangerous enemies were stalking through the dark . . . tigers and leopards.

It was on a pitch-black night during a raging storm that a man was killed in his field. His death was never satisfactorily explained, although I had a pretty definite idea about what had really happened. It may or may not have been the work of a tiger, but in no time at all that is what everyone believed had killed him.

That was the first time I was left to guard the fields on my own—a part of the bargain I had never thought of. Yet who could blame the nightwatchmen? When a man-eating tiger prowls the fields why should they guard another man's crops for the equivalent of £3 a month? At first, as I moved though the dark and whispering forests, a constant companion was fear; for, beside the unpredictable wild boars and a possible man-eating tiger, a tigress with two cubs was known to be wandering the estate and a pair of mating leopards had their home somewhere near Monkey's Folly.

I little realized then that this was just the first spell of what has since become a simple routine chore: guarding the fields at night whenever some unusual animal or occurrence has scared the nightwatchmen away. Since that time I have been on my own so often that I have forgotten many of the reasons that kept the night watchmen at home. I do, however, remember the terrible cries of the 'human demon' which eventually turned out to be a bear badly burned in a forest fire. The 'singing tigress' too, she was also an evil spirit in animal guise which lived in a tree near the well. Her peculiar vocal efforts were certainly unusual but actually nothing more than a long drawn-out love call. Rather different from the rest was the rabid jackal. This kept us worried for a whole night with screams that were so much out of this world that we could not help wondering whether the forest devils were in fact so imaginary after all.

These days there is also another reason which can keep a farmer close to a rifle if his herds of cattle and the men who guard them are to be safe. Half the stories in this book are about animals which have been wounded and not followed up. This is a state of affairs rapidly going from bad to worse. During the last ten years times have changed considerably and there is now little or no check on illegal shooting. Indeed, the present position is so appalling and the slaughter so great that in a very few years, unless something drastic is done quickly,

India will have lost forever much of her finest fauna. That I know has been said many times before and as yet, no animal has actually become extinct; just why it is likely to come true this time, and perhaps very soon, will be found in the chapter on the Lonely Tiger.

A great deal of this illegal shooting is done on forest roads at night from sneaking jeeps. As the animals show up in the headlights, they are shot at by perhaps as many as four gunners that blast away together. But even against such a withering fire it is surprising how many animals get away wounded. A large number of them of course die in agony perhaps a day or a week later; but others survive—usually to live out their lives as hopeless cripples. When this happens to either a tiger or a leopard there is a real danger that the victim will turn man-eater if painful wounds at last stop it from catching a more agile prey.

Yes, here in the jungle that other side of the penny may turn up at any time. But I'm not complaining; if there's a good and sufficient reason to go out and kill, my conscience is clear and gives the hunting urge full rein. There are no qualms about pulling a trigger then: a wounded animal, be it dangerous or not, is one of the most pathetic sights I know and I would rather see it dead.

Mandikhera,
P.O. Piparia MP,
India 1960.

THE ODD CHANCE . . .

Some years ago, when I was showing a friend round our jungles, he suddenly turned to me and asked why I had come out with only a walking stick. 'In a place like this, isn't there every chance of meeting a tiger?' he added.

I do not think he really believed me when I told him that the chances of meeting a tiger were practically nil and that it was possible to walk through the jungles every day for years without ever seeing one.

'But—' he persisted '—what would you do now without a rifle if one suddenly came charging towards us?'

I was not able to convince him. Nor was I really surprised that I could not. The idea that a tiger is always a dangerous animal and liable to attack on sight is one shared by nearly everyone unfamiliar with the jungles. In fact, however, the tiger is very seldom dangerous until provoked and in its normal state does not molest man. Indeed, the tiger wants so little to do with man that it will always stay out of his sight if it possibly can.

Yet, in a way, that friend of mine was right. The odd chance does occasionally turn up and you meet a tiger bent on mischief even though it has not been provoked in the ordinary way. But just how rare that chance really is may be gauged from my own experience. For more than ten years I have walked through the jungles every day and that odd chance for me has turned up just once. . .

It was on a stifling evening at the end of our first hot weather. Tea had been over about an hour and I was sitting on the veranda when Babs reminded me that the meat in the larder was low. Almost as she spoke I heard peafowl calling from the direction of Stony Ford, a crossing over a nullah some quarter of a mile away. A few minutes later, I had left the house with a 12-bore and a pocketful of cartridges. As I set off towards the sound of the calling birds, angry black clouds were building up above the distant hills; the rains were due to break at any moment.

I was making for a strip of scrub jungle that fringes the bank of a large nullah. In there, if the peafowl eluded me, I might later put up some pig or come across a barking deer or a chital stag. Through this jungle runs a smaller nullah that joins the larger one. This is about ten feet wide and some six feet deep and I dropped down to its sandy bed when I reached it. The banks are lined with many kinds of jungle trees. That day, some of these were already in full leaf while others were performing that yearly miracle of producing delicate little leaves and buds from a rock-like soil seemingly devoid of a drop of moisture.

Peafowl are difficult to surprise, but a stalk along the sandy bed of the nullah could be made in silence. A little farther down I hoped to find some of the birds feeding and get a shot before they could fly out of range. I started to creep forward and kept going for about ten minutes. Then, while edging round a bend, I was suddenly stopped dead.

Just in front of me and apparently asleep under a patch of

shade was a large leopard stretched on the sand. But there was something wrong. A closer look showed that its attitude was unnatural. The head was twisted grotesquely and one forepaw was slightly bent and held drunkenly in the air. The leopard was dead.

As I started to approach it, my nose told me that it had been dead for some time. A swarm of blue flies buzzed up as I came nearer and wafted the sickly-sweet smell of death more strongly to my nostrils. Something had eaten a small part of the hindquarters and the sand all round the leopard was wildly churned; the sand was too dry to show what animal had been feeding.

I began to look around me and almost at once spotted something else. A little farther down the nullah, hard against one bank, were the remains of what had once been a chital stag. All that was left now was the head, a few pieces of skin and splintered bone, and two almost whole ribs.

Both animals had been dead for about two days, and I was just beginning to wonder what had happened when I noticed that a small flame-of-the-forest tree had fallen across the nullah some ten yards farther down. It was blocking the nullah completely, but starting not far in front of it I could see in the sand the mark of a drag which disappeared into the collage of the fallen tree; something heavy had been dragged through to the other side. I went up to the tree and, after tearing away some of the leaves and smaller branches, saw something black lying within two yards of me. It was the dead body of a huge wild boar.

I climbed over the tree and looked down at it. The mask was set in a ferocious snarl, and the one tush I could see was stained brown with congealed blood. The remains were fresh, the meat hardly tainted, but the body of the boar had been horribly ripped and torn and once again a little had been eaten off the hindquarters. This was the work of a tiger, and if that bloodstained tush meant what I thought it did, the tiger had not had the fight all his own way.

As I got up from examining the boar, I suddenly realized that the jungle around me was strangely quiet. I looked up at the trees for vultures and found not a single one in sight. The truth came to me the next second. Somewhere very close at hand the tiger was lying up. It *had* to be: with the dead leopard lying pretty much in the open, that was the only explanation for no vultures.

It was now just six o'clock and a little darker than usual. The black clouds I had noticed when leaving the house had crept up overhead and muffled thunder was vibrating in the stifling air. All at once I made for the bank and climbed quickly out of the nullah: its sandy bed now was an unhealthy spot for this was a likely time for the tiger to return for a feed. Once at the top of the bank, I moved to a clump of saplings and stood listening. The jungle here was still scrub but very thick; the previous year it had been cut over and now, with the amazing rapidity with which the forests revive, the old stumps had sent up several shoots to a height of many feet. Visibility in any direction was only a few yards.

As I stood on the bank listening, I was a little uneasy. To be so near the kills at a time when the tiger might come back to feed was asking for trouble, and I should have liked to know if it had already either seen or heard me. I was still thinking about that when, without the slightest warning, the tiger appeared about five yards in front of me.

It came from behind a small cluster of teak like a conjurer's illusion. At first it did not see me for it was moving obliquely away, but I must have given some slight start of surprise which caused it to stop and turn. I saw then that it was a tigress and she was looking straight at me. I can still see those eyes even today; but why I remember them so clearly is not because they held the threat of sudden death, but because they were vacant and not seeing me at all. I might have been some usual piece of jungle scenery, and when the tigress had gazed for several seconds she turned calmly away and then passed out of sight behind some cover.

As she went I saw that she was plastered with dried mud and along her left flank ran a long, bloody gash; and she was moving with a marked limp.

To this day I cannot understand why that tigress's sudden arrival caused me so much surprise. She so obviously *had* to be somewhere close. Yet when she came I was caught completely off my guard and made no effort to bring her down. As she moved away, an easier target could hardly have been imagined. It was the sort of chance sportsmen often dream of but so seldom get in reality. Perhaps, though, that little jungle God who looks after fools was tapping on my shoulder; for had I fired instinctively it might well have been, for *two* reasons, the last trigger I ever squeezed.

The moment after the tigress disappeared from sight I recovered my wits. It had been an odd encounter and there was much I still did not understand; but there was no doubt that she was a badly crippled animal and if I was quick there was still a good chance to put her out of her pain. After the blistering heat of the day, she should now be making for water. She had certainly gone in the right direction: there was a pool in a larger nullah about fifty yards away. If I could surprise her there she would be a sitting shot from the bank above it.

I gave her a minute's start and then followed. About twenty yards from where I was standing there is a little clearing among the trees; on the other side of it the ground rises sleepily and is covered with bushes and small trees. When I came into this I stopped and looked around. There was no sign of the tigress.

I was about to go on when I glanced down at my weapon. The next second I got a nasty shock when I realized that, aided and abetted by my bad memory, I had been acting like a lunatic ever since finding that butcher's shop in the small nullah. In the excitement of the moment I had forgotten two things: one that I was carrying a shotgun, and the other that it was loaded in the left barrel with number 6 and with buck-shot in the right.

However, it was a mistake easily rectified even though I am never happy with a shotgun against a tiger. In the handful of cartridges I had brought out there was one 'lethal ball'. I broke the gun and took out the number 6 and then fished about in my pocket until I found the case I wanted.

The tigress's roar seemed to burst in my ear. Then I heard her crashing towards me from the high ground a little to my right. The next second she hurtled into view and with a mighty bound landed in the clearing some thirty paces in front of me.

The shock and surprise were so complete that the ball cartridge fell from my fingers as I was putting it in the breech. I know now that this mishap undoubtedly saved my life; for if the gun had been loaded I should have used it at once and before I'd had time to appreciate the situation.

It took me perhaps fifteen seconds to realize that the animal before me now was not the tigress but a tiger. That he was bent on mischief there was no doubt. The moment he landed on his feet, he whipped about to face me and then began weaving quickly from side to side across my front. At the same time he was throwing up his head and shattering the air with bellowing roars. Then he began to make quick feint attacks. He'd dart in crouching low to the ground with his hindquarters slightly raised and ears laid hard against his head. All at once he would check with his lips mouthing a vicious snarl that spat out between gleaming fangs. The next second he would break his feint with a great sideways leap to start weaving and roaring again.

At any second that tiger was coming in. He was playing like a cat with a mouse and the real attack could not be delayed long. Each time he threatened, my eyes went to the end of his tail. The moment that flickered he would spring. All this time I had been creeping slowly backwards, fascinated by that prancing yellow body. The shotgun still hung open over my left arm. Should I suddenly snap it shut and try for his head with the buckshot in the right barrel?

Before I could make up my mind I saw something that ruled this idea right out. From the corner of my eye I had spotted the tigress. She was under a small tree just a few yards to my right sitting up like a big cat before a fire. On her face was a pleased smile as she watched the scene before her.

When I found her so close I suddenly knew what was really going on. These two were mating. That would explain her extraordinary behaviour earlier when she had ignored me so near the kills; for it is not uncommon when the female's in season to find her going about in a kind of dazed, ecstatic trance.

After that diversion for the fraction of a second, my eyes snapped back to the tiger. There was no ecstatic trance about him! He was right out for business and getting more excited every moment. This encounter was just what he wanted: a chance to show-off before his sweetheart, and if that charnel house in the nullah was anything to go by this tiger had had some practice.

I was still moving slowly backwards, when something prodded me in the small of the back. I whipped round to find that it was a small tree. I had reached the limit of the clearing. Very carefully, I edged round the slender trunk. At least it was a stick of cover, but even as I got behind it I knew that the game could not go on much longer. The tiger *must* come in now: he knew as well as I did that behind me lay the jungle and the safety of the trees.

Help came from the most unexpected quarter. A thin tongue of lightning flickered down in a brilliant violent flash. Hard on it came a deafening crash of thunder from right overhead. It stopped the tiger dead in his tracks. Then came the rain. At first just a few large drops spattered against my hat and bare arms. Then, to another crash of thunder, a deluge roared down from the leaden sky.

A solid sheet of water was suddenly cascading before my eyes and soon splashing up from the ground in a fine mist. Quickly taking advantage of this heaven-sent diversion, I moved farther behind my tree. But the tiger had given up. As the rain rattled and bounced off his streaming back it seemed as though all the ardour had soaked right out of him. Watching him closely I put another buckshot cartridge in the empty chamber and then slowly closed the gun; as it snicked shut I slipped off the safety-catch.

But the game was over. With a great shake of his rain-soaked body the tiger suddenly wheeled about and then trotted away. Almost at once he was joined by the tigress. The last I saw of them they were bounding away together towards some broken land where they probably found shelter in a cave. . .

That was undoubtedly my lucky day for several reasons. Firstly, if I had met the tiger instead of the tigress near the small nullah I do not think he would have hesitated for a single second. He would have come for me at once because I was far too near his kills and a tiger's temper is always short whenever he is mixed up with a tigress.

The tiger, of course, had killed that leopard. As I see it, the tiger must have surprised the leopard soon after *the leopard* had killed that chital stag. But the leopard—and some are very bold—must have refused to give way over his own kill. Then the tiger went for him, not so much for the possession of the carcase but to show off to his mate. The tiger had attacked the boar, too; but it is not unlikely that the boar proved such a tough antagonist that the tigress had waded in to help. In the fracas she got that long gash down her side.

The two reasons that might have proved fatal if I had shot at the tigress? Nothing is more certain than the fact that I should have given her the choke barrel if I had fired the moment she appeared—and merely peppered her with number 6. That would have been enough to bring her straight at me. After that, from such close quarters, I doubt whether I should have killed her with a single charge of buckshot in time. But even if I had, there was still the tiger about which I still knew nothing. I don't think I would have got away a second time if he had caught me unawares bending over the dead body of his lady love.

THE THIRD KILL

This was the strangest encounter with a tiger I've had. The most alarming, too, though the fear that gripped me so suddenly in the darkness had in fact little to do with the stealthy arrival of the tiger. That was something I had been expecting. The scream was not, and when it ripped through the night it caught me completely by surprise. Now tigers don't scream, and there was nothing within miles that could have made such a noise for it was unlike anything I had ever heard in the jungle before. When it came again I began to think of all the stories I'd heard about the forest devils. . .

To start with, however, this was one of those occasions that promised a fruitless vigil. Indeed, the signs seemed so set against success that I nearly did not go. What put me off first was the time of day that news of the kill came in, for it was three-thirty in the afternoon before I heard of it. That meant little time for any arrangements; the kill was five miles away and with the cold weather well advanced the nights were drawing in. By the time I arrived it would be nearly dark.

In the end, common sense made me go. This was a chance I could not really afford to ignore even though the odds against success seemed heavy. I was thinking of our own stock. A cattle-killing tiger works over a large area, and this one might easily move across to the estate and do considerable damage before he offered another chance.

Twenty minutes after the news came in, I was striding along the dusty track to Mogra. I reached the village within an hour and was met by the headman and a small crowd of men. A few minutes were enough to hear the main details. The kill had been made soon after midday and the tiger had then dragged the dead cow into a strip of jungle through which ran a small ravine. At about two o'clock, the carcase had been found by four of the villagers who had built a machan in a tree near by. When this was finished the kill had been tied down and then one of the men had come across to call me.

That all sounded pretty straightforward. It was the proper drill with nothing forgotten and, if the machan had been well concealed, the chances now were much brighter for this was something I had not reckoned on finding ready.

'Anything else?' I asked, getting up from my chair on the headman's small veranda.

There was a short silence. Then, rather slowly, the headman said, 'No. . . that was just about all.' That warned me at once that I had not heard the whole story and that something was deliberately being held back.

I was not really surprised. By now experience of the jungle men had taught me that they will often withhold some vital piece of information if it is likely to stop you trying for a tiger which is worrying their cattle. It is usually something they think might prevent the tiger returning to the kill. But, as confirmed optimists with quite a sense of humour, they will cheerfully let you sit up all night on what they know will almost certainly be a waste of time.

Luckily, these jungle men are very simple. In cases like

this, if they are in fact holding anything back, a few seemingly artless questions nearly always brings it out.

My third question, which asked whether anyone had been near the machan since the four men came away, unearthed the first clue. After another short silence, the headman's reply was just a short grunt followed by a sharp hiss as he sent a stream of betel juice sailing across the veranda to the ground outside. The jungle man's way of avoiding a direct answer. It's a gesture that can mean either yes or no, and if you're too polite to press you have to form your own opinion.

I've learnt to press. And when I did the headman reluctantly added that the entire village herd of cattle had been all around the machan less than half an hour before.

It was not an uncommon story. Indian herds are usually tended by small boys that are just as curious and naughty as any other small boys the world over. The two that had been in charge of this one were no exceptions: the temptation 'to see the dead cow' had proved too much and against the strictest orders to stay clear they had driven their cattle home past the machan.

Once that was out there was yet another short and rather embarrassed silence which suggested that I still had not heard the worst. I asked the headman again if there was anything else. Before he replied, another stream of betel hissed through the air. Then he slowly admitted that, as a matter of fact there was: the herd had suddenly stampeded near the spot where the dead cow lay and had then raced home in a swirling cloud of dust.

That seemed to be all I had not heard at the start. It was quite enough, but as the two young cowherds might have had some more information they had not thought important enough to pass on to their elders, I asked to see them.

The headman laughed. 'Those young rascals have not come back. They will have run over to their grandmother's place at Bandakhera for they well know what is waiting them here after disobeying orders. We won't see *them* until tomorrow, but they will find our memories just as good then as they are now.'

It was not a promising start. The hope that had surged up when I heard about the ready-made machan now ebbed away at the thought of all those cattle and the two boys trampling round the kill. Before that the tiger had undoubtedly been lying close by it; but now, if he had an ounce of caution, he would be many miles away and stalking something else for his supper.

Even so, I was going to sit. With a tiger you can never be sure. Some stick to the rules while others tear up the book; it all depends on the kind of animal it is and what experience has taught it. . .

▪

Four men with axes over their shoulders were ready to take me the remaining mile to where the kill lay. We took the first three-quarters of it fast; then the leading man suddenly stopped and pointed ahead: 'The machan', he said, 'is just below that big pipul tree over there. From here on we will go more quietly.'

He was just going on when I stopped him. We were standing at the edge of some grassland dotted with scrub trees and bushes. Over the tops of these, some four hundred yards ahead, was a giant pipul towering above a patch of jungle. If that marked the machan there was no reason why I should not go on alone. It was now getting late and a hungry tiger would be thinking about food. In spite of everything that had happened, our quarry might already be on the kill or somewhere near it.

When the men had left me I checked the rifle and then spent a few minutes listening to the jungle. The evening was very still. The only sounds about me came from birds getting ready for bed. None of them was excited; there was no big cat on the prowl around here.

The going through the grass was dead silent and fifteen minutes later the patch of jungle and the giant pipul lay fifty yards ahead. I had crossed the grass without incident and nowhere seen or heard any sign of a tiger. I stopped again to listen. All was quiet, but just as I started to move on a sudden movement caught the corner of my eye.

I was still surrounded with scrub trees and bushes, and there was not a breath of wind. Yet, the lower leaves on a clump of bushes some way over to my left had suddenly shaken.

I half turned and stared across at them. The movement had stopped. Even so my eyes raced over and around them for a full minute trying to pick out something that did not belong. All at once it was there. A spot of reddish-brown flicked my gaze to the right and a little behind the bushes.

A large animal was crouched in the long grass.

The sight of it had been so sudden that I braced instinctively to meet a charge. But the thing in the grass didn't move. Not a flick from a tail nor the twitch of an ear. I stared harder . . . then a dab of black and a fleck of white told me what it was.

A black nose and the white of an eye staring at the sky.

I crept forward until the thing lay at my feet. A dead calf, its head twisted grotesquely across its body and in the neck, just behind the ears, were the fang marks of a tiger.

So the headman *had* held something back after all. His 'full-grown cow' was a calf. That, however, was typical: all tigers are invariably of gigantic size and their victims always the best and biggest animals in the herd. Now the size of a victim of course does not matter and I was not worried about that. But here was a situation I had not foreseen, and it was one that now put me in a tricky position. The tiger must have been to the kill already, broken the rope holding it down, and then—when he had been dragging it away from the machan—my sudden arrival had disturbed him.

I began to look about me for signs of the drag. There was not a single mark or other sign, and I had just come to the conclusion that the tiger must have been carrying the calf bodily, when the truth sprang at me from the ground. The whole story was in the trampled grass around my feet.

This was the spot where the tiger had stampeded the herd. That seemed to upset my first theory completely, and if what I guessed now was right the tiger had done something more than just stampede the herd. The calf in the grass was his second kill.

What about the message from the shaking leaves on the bush? That puzzled me for a few moments more until I realized that little had changed and that the message could still mean that the killer was very near. The only difference was that the tiger—if indeed, he had been there to move the leaves—had not been dragging the first kill away from the machan but just coming up to feed on the second.

The ground was too hard to show pug marks, and none of the leaves and twigs on the bush yielded any of the tell-tale yellow hairs a tiger might have left behind. There was no clue and he may or may not have been here when I arrived. The chances were about even. Warm air rising from the ground might have moved those leaves; so might a bird I had not seen; or it might have been just a plain illusion conjured up by a failing light.

As there was no definite sign here of the tiger's recent presence, I decided to stalk on to the first kill. Over the scrub just in front of me, I could see the giant pipul dead ahead. Bearing on that I went quietly forward and when the grass ended at the fringe of the jungle, I stopped. There was no sound of anything moving and no sound of a tiger tearing at a kill.

A little to my right a game-path led away into the jungle. I moved towards it and then started slowly along it. After thirty yards, I spotted the machan in the branches of a stunted tree. A few more careful steps and I saw a white cow stiff on the ground below it. No part of the carcase had been eaten.

Under the trees, it was now unpleasantly dark. I stood still once again to listen, but the only sounds were the last notes of an occasional bird and a few early cicadas tuning up. That short period of silence which falls on the jungle just before nightfall was starting. I looked at the dead cow and then at the machan almost immediately above it. My heart sank. *What a hell of a mess!* Two kills about eighty yards apart and only one machan . . . and that a bare nine feet up the tree and looking like a gigantic crow's nest.

There seemed to be only one thing to do. The thought of doing it, though, really alarmed me. But as it was very probable that the tiger had heard the men putting up the machan, the second kill was the one he would go for if he came back. So, as I was going to spend the night in the machan and I wanted him to come to the dead cow, he would have to be denied that calf.

I ended up in a lather of cold sweat. The calf had been heavy and dragging it over the carpet of crisp leaves under the trees had been a real ordeal. The noise had been appalling and sounded like a direct invitation to the tiger to come and see what was happening to his dinner. At last, it lay beside the dead cow. Then, after tying it down, I tossed my haversack into the machan and climbed up after it.

As soon as I was settled, I lit a pipe. After dragging that calf my nerves badly needed soothing. As a rule, though, I don't smoke when I first get into a machan and only light up when the business on hand is finished. On this occasion, however, I was quite convinced that it wouldn't matter if I smoked till dawn.

No sensible tiger was likely to offer any chances tonight. True, the rightful owner of the kills might yet return to see whether the coast was clear, if he had not seen me near the dead calf and had been far enough away to miss all that noise later. But one glance at the heap of dead cows below the machan must surely keep him at a respectful distance.

By the time my pipe had smoked half-way down, the last of the light had gone. Fifteen minutes later, the night was as black as pitch. Now, even the nearest trees had merged into a solid wall of darkness; the only glimmer of light was above my head where the faintly luminous sky filtered through the leaves; all I could see of the ground below was the dim blur of the white cow.

Suddenly, I put away my pipe. Without warning the old thrill of waiting for a tiger had come surging through me. To be sure, I hadn't forgotten the noise of the drag, the two kills tied together or even the possibility that the tiger had seen me just before I found the calf. But while sitting there, smoking, I had been looking at the other side of the picture.

What reason had I got to suppose that the tiger had ever been anywhere near me? After the disturbance in the afternoon, was it not more likely that all this time he had been a considerable distance away and so unaware of my interference with his kills? There was something to back that theory up. A tiger moving by day invariably excites a lot of comment from both birds and beasts. Yet, from the moment I had started to cross the grass until now, not a living thing had screamed a warning.

If that supposition was right, it could of course mean, too, that the tiger had gone for good—scared away by the two boys and the herd. It was now that I began to wonder for the first time what sort of animal this really was, for he could be either confirmed cattle-killer or just a normal tiger.

The men at the village had told me that this tiger was a new arrival and that the kill in the morning had been a casual one. That surmise I had been ready to accept: those men knew all the local cattle-thieves well, their areas of operation and, as often as not, even their pug marks. But the village had not known of the second kill. That altered the situation quite a bit even though it still didn't make this tiger an old cattle-thief. However, the circumstances did suggest something else—something that could be the most dangerous animal of all—a freshly wounded tiger just starting out to find the easiest prey to catch.

That might well be the answer. I fell to thinking of all the illegal shooting that was going on and of how seldom a dangerous animal was followed up when wounded. I remembered, too, a similar setup once before to the one I was on now. A sudden brace of kills in the morning and then a doubt in my mind that the tiger would come back once I was up in the machan. At eleven o'clock it had come back roaring and berserk from hunger. It knew I was up in a tree and the only thing that kept it on the ground was a recent bullet wound through the right foreleg.

In the darkness I began to feel about the machan. The rough platform felt secure but it was much larger than I would have made it for myself. The real trouble was the screening: horribly untidy with patches too thick and some too thin. A suspicious tiger wouldn't like it, and he'd like it even less if he had just been wounded by a bullet fired from some similar-looking mass up a tree.

I looked at the ground. The vague white patch made by the cow was only some nine feet away. The machan was far too low. If the tiger was in fact a wounded one and in the mood for revenge, he wouldn't even need to spring. Just an easy reach up and he could claw the sitting duck from its nest.

I should have liked to climb higher up the tree. But to start moving now was unwise. A tiger comes quietly, and his sharp eyes and ears might already be around watching and listening. Safer to keep still. The ground was strewn with dry leaves and with a grain of luck I would hear him coming.

It was now nine o'clock and getting cold. The chilly air and my disturbing thoughts had started me shivering. I reached out slowly for the haversack; what I needed was some hot coffee. I drank two cups and then settled down again to listen to the jungle.

It was a still night and sounds were carrying well. In the village over a mile away, I could hear a barking dog and the low throbbing of a drum; from the mangers came the tinkle of cattle-bells. But near about me there was nothing but the normal sounds of a jungle night—millions of chirping insects, whispering leaves, small reptiles and rodents rustling over the leafy carpet, the monotonous croak of a bull-frog from a pool in the ravine.

■

It is now a little after midnight and really chilly. The long watch has left me cramped and sleepy so I feel for the thermos again. My hands are cold and clumsy; as the cap unscrews there is a slight squeak. The next second, I can hear the pounding of my heart and my head is twisted sharply to the right to listen behind. The tiny sound I have just heard was like a crisp leaf crunched slowly under a heavy paw.

There it is again. The sound has come from right behind me and not far away. I'm sure now that some animal is creeping up to the machan. *What is it?* For a few seconds I am not sure. Hyenas and jackals creep up to kills too and can be an unmitigated nuisance. But there's an indefinable something which now tells what the animal is and a moment later I know. Near the back of the machan is a tiger.

In the slowest of slow time, I get the flask out of the way. The barrel of the rifle is resting between my feet with the butt lying across my thigh. My hands creep towards it and grasp the forepart and grip. Inch by inch I bring it up to my shoulder with the muzzle pointing towards the kills. In this position I wait with my ears straining for the next sound.

My brain is a whirling medley of racing thoughts: How long has the tiger been so close? Did he hear that squeak from the flask? Or has he just arrived—perhaps suspicious but without any real clue to the danger above his kills?

The tension mounts as the minutes creep by. The glowing dial of my watch is ticking them off—five have passed. The tiger has not made another sound. The strain of listening is beginning to tell and a faint singing has started in my ears. But I must listen even harder; these are critical moments and to be one jump ahead of him I have to know which one of three things he is doing . . . going off scared . . . creeping up to the kill . . . *or getting ready for a roaring smack at the machan.*

The answer comes suddenly from out of the blackness to my left. A whispered warning that the tiger is still near the machan. My ears catch the faint *swish!* as a body slides past leaves. Then a slight rustle—like a brittle leaf brushed gently aside by a creeping paw.

The duel is on. The tiger has now moved over to the left and it seems as though the danger has passed. I sense that he suspects the machan of holding something that should not be there. *But he is not sure.* So he is setting out to make certain and until he is, he will keep his distance. He won't hurry. It may be an hour or more before he is satisfied, and all the time he will be circling around with frequent stops to watch and listen. To outwit him, there must not be the slightest sound nor the tiniest movement.

The dim glow of my watch is the only thing I can see. It says that thirty minutes have crawled by since that last rustle. The tiger has not betrayed himself again. Neither have I. The strain is mounting; my limbs are cramped and aching, the temptation to move them almost unbearable. But the certainty that the tiger is somewhere near in the darkness below, taut as a steel spring, keeps me sitting as still as a rock.

Without warning the tension snaps. From some way out in front of the machan, I suddenly hear heavy pads crunching boldly over leaves. *Here he comes!* The ruthless inspection is over and by some freak of luck those sharp eyes have been deceived by the untidy mass of the machan in the branches above the kills. Now the tiger is coming to feed.

He was farther off than I imagined. But he is coming on steadily though he is moving slowly. Now he seems about forty yards off and still slightly left of me. All at once he stops. As he does, my left thumb tightens on the switch of the torch mounted on the barrel of the rifle. *Has something at last warned him? Should I try to take him now?*

Before I can make up my mind, he is moving again and still coming towards the machan. That slight check was probably a final look round when he picked up the blur of the kills, for the second after he moves the night is split by a growling grunt of pleasure.

Then it came. A high-pitched shriek suddenly screams out of the night from somewhere not far beyond the kills. It catches my taut nerves so completely unawares that it jerks me upright from my crouched position on the machan. The abrupt movement shivers the tree and rattles the branches.

As the shriek dies away, I hear the tiger whip round on the loose leaves. There's a shattering roar . . . then he's streaking away to the right like a scalded cat.

The noise of the tiger's flight has faded into the distance and a sudden hush has fallen on the jungle. Even the cicadas are stunned. Only one sound is breaking the eerie silence. It is the pounding of my heart beating out a question: *What out of hell was that?*

It was the cry of no jungle bird nor beast, and in all my experience I had never heard anything like it before, either by day or night. In spite of myself my hands are trembling, the sweat oozing from the palms as they grip the rifle.

The inky blackness suddenly seems more intense and

the sighing of the wind holds a sinister note. It sounds like whispering voices. With an effort I chase away the vision of banshee fairies and tell myself there's some natural and obvious explanation. *But what?* race my thoughts. The distorted screech of some night bird? Terror twisting the cry of some small animal suddenly frightened?

It's no use. I can't fool myself at all. Whatever made that noise was no natural denizen of the forest. To back that up, I have the best authority in the world. It scared the tiger, too. *He* didn't know what it was—and that's an animal so steeped in jungle lore that he would not have misunderstood for a single second the cry of any bird or beast screamed normally or not.

With that unearthly shriek still needing an explanation, I soon find my imagination running wild. *Forest devils and evil spirits!* Over the years, I have unconsciously absorbed many of the superstitions all our jungle folk believe in. I find myself reminding the harvesters to break a coconut before reaping the crops; and as a matter of course I give my shikaris a black cock to appease the jungle gods whenever my hunting luck is out.

Have I been utterly wrong all these years? In reality, do these simple people of the jungle know more than I do? To those two questions I may soon have the answers, for the black night suddenly seems much colder and the whispering in the trees is getting louder; above my head monstrous shapes keep forming as the leaves wave against the dark luminous velvet of the sky.

WOW-ou! WOW-ou! The spell breaks suddenly. That was the high-pitched alarm call of a chital hind about half a mile away. This is something I understand and I sit forward waiting for it to come again. It does—three times. As the last call dies away, it seems to me that it marks the end of my tiger, for the hind is surely calling at him.

Another cup of coffee chases away the last of the devils. As the hot brew seeps through me, I am resolving to find out at the crack of dawn what made that shriek. It will probably turn out to be something so ordinary that I will for ever be ashamed when I think of this night.

I feel in my pockets again for pipe and tobacco. The flare of a match won't matter now and a smoke will round off the coffee. As I pack the bowl I realize that I'm very tired and for the first time the machan does not seem too big. When the pipe is finished I'll doze. I find the matches and the wind blows the first one out. I strike another, shielding it in my cupped hands. It flares brightly and catches. But it never lights my pipe. For, as the flame flickers through the darkness, that piercing shriek rips through the night again.

The match drops flaming to my lap as this fresh shock sets me clutching the edge of the machan. A moment later, a tingling wave of near-panic is surging through me as shriek after shriek comes screaming out of the darkness. It's like a human soul in mortal terror suffering all the tortures of hell. I listen while the blood slowly curdles in my veins.

Suddenly the shrieks stop as abruptly as they started. There's a moment of silence which is followed by a choking gurgle. Then comes a new sound. It's scarcely audible, a sort of low sighing that rises and falls gently but erratic and fast. It's coming from perhaps fifty or sixty yards away in front of the machan. I can't locate it exactly; but with everything I've got I'm trying to identify it with something that is flesh and blood.

But at the end of another ten minutes I still don't know what it is even though my ears are strained as never before.

Yet . . . something about it now is familiar. It's a sound very like another I've heard many times before. I shake my head in an effort to sharpen my ears. The sound comes again and it is just as familiar. *But how the devil can it be that?* The very idea is fantastic for I'm quite alone in the middle of a dark jungle. But the fancy persists, and now a small nagging voice it whispering in my ear that what I'm hearing cannot be anything else but a child sobbing its heart out.

I listen for another thirty seconds. The sounds are getting fainter and threatening to die away. It doesn't make sense. It simply *can't* be true. Yet, unless the strain of the last few hours has played some odd trick with my mind, there is someone on the ground not far from the front of the machan.

For a few moments I consider getting down and then going to explore on foot. But at the back of my mind there is still a doubt and as it is never wise to play about near a tiger's kill in the dark, I decide to call out instead. I cup my hands about my mouth and then send out a low *Anybody there?*

A stifled scream answers me. Then comes a low, babbled stream of words. *Words!* At last I'm sure for there is no mistaking the human voice. I call again louder and ask who it is. The babbling rises abruptly to a high piping treble which sounds like a frantic prayer of entreaty.

A moment later I'm out of the machan and swinging to the ground. That piping treble has suddenly rung a bell. As I stride towards the sounds, the spare torch is cutting a bright path across the carpet of leaves spread over the forest floor. *What a blind fool I've been!* I can only hope that I am not too late for I know now what I'm going to find.

The sobbing draws me to a patch of lantana clustered round the gnarled trunk of a spreading kossum. The white beam flickers over it and then stops on a gap beaten in towards the tree. A few steps more and I see him. Ringed in the brilliant circle of light is a frightened face with tears streaming down the cheeks. Its owner is a small boy in a ragged shirt huddled against the trunk.

He is shivering violently with fright and cold. I kneel down and play the torch over him. As far as I can see he is not hurt, and in answer to my whispered question he stammers out that he can walk. A few minutes later we are up in the machan where I wrap him in my coat and then pour out a steaming cup of coffee. When he has gulped it down, I hand him another. Then he tells me his name is Bali and he is one of the two cowherds who 'ran home to Grannie'.

Slowly, as the hot brew warms him up, his story comes out. When the herd stampeded he had been in the middle of it and 'the big bull Raja' had knocked him down. A moment later he got a stunning crack on the head. He was a little vague about how long he had been 'out'; but he remembered coming to and then lying still and trying to collect his thoughts. They came back slowly for he felt sick and his head was splitting. Then the memory of what had happened and the appalling truth of where he was crashed through the pain. Sheer terror suddenly gave him the strength to dive into the lantana. Which was lucky; for not much later the whisperings of the jungle had so paralysed his senses that he could neither move nor shout. He had heard my arrival which I thought had been so silent; he had heard me dragging the calf, too, but with his mind full of tigers he had not dared to look out to see what was going on.

When the tiger did at last arrive, he heard it plainly. For quite a while it had remained close to the lantana and that grunting growl of pleasure had exploded only a few yards from where he sat. That was the last straw. What he had dreaded most all through those long frightening hours suddenly became a reality and there was not a doubt in his mind that the brute was looking just for him. That terrible certainty at last unsealed his lips and forced out that first shriek of despair.

When Bali has told his story, I ask him why he did not answer my call from the machan.

'I thought you were the tiger,' he said simply.

'The tiger . . . ?'

'Of course. Everybody knows that all tigers are devils and can change themselves into anything they choose. So when he couldn't find me I knew he had become a tree devil and was calling me over to be eaten.'

I don't tell him that he wasn't the only one thinking of devils. Instead, I give him a handful of the big 'bulls' eyes' I always take to stop me coughing when sitting up. Bali starts to chew them, but now that he is feeling snug and secure he is eager to go on talking. Just now, however, I don't want to hear any more from him because I want to think. A disturbing thought has begun to form in my mind and I want to examine it carefully. But even with his mouth full of bulls' eyes, Bali goes babbling on: Would the tiger come back? And if it does, can he hand me 'the big bullets' as I fire them off?

Surprisingly, his chatter stops when I tell him that the tiger will never return so long as he is talking. But even with his tongue stilled there is only a comparative silence in the machan. The trouble now is the bulls' eyes. Bali is enjoying them, and I begin to wonder whether they can hear him crunching back at the village.

But I don't try to stop him. By now I have thrown out that disturbing thought as improbable and am back to believing that the night's excitement is over. After all that has happened it would be a bold tiger indeed that came back again. So let Bali chew on; he can't, after all, have so very many bulls' eyes left. . .

■

The tiger came back about an hour before dawn. I had fallen into a light sleep when a sound in the distance woke me. For a few moments I was not sure. *Had I dreamed it?* Then it came again—the deep-throated *AOO-OO UFF!* of a tiger coming to feed and not caring a damn who knew it.

The call comes twice more and each time it is closer to the machan. As I shake the sleep from my eyes and reach for the rifle a weight pressing against my left knee reminds me of Bali. He's fast asleep with his head over the front edge of the machan. I wake him gently and then whisper that the tiger is coming; then I push him behind me with a stern warning to keep good and quiet.

The tiger is coming on fast. Soon after his second call, I hear him swishing through the brush some way out on the right. This time it seems that nothing is going to stop him and he is heading straight for the kills. Bali is pressing close behind me and trembling with excitement. Except for that he is sitting as still as a rock and just as mute. The tiger is now on the dead leaves and crunching steadily nearer. If only there was a little more light I might be able to see him; but the dawn is still an hour away and what is left of the night is still as black as pitch. Suddenly the tiger checks. He seems now to be only a few yards away. Then I hear him move again as he starts to pad forward with more caution.

He has stopped behind the machan. Fifteen electric seconds pass and I can almost feel his eyes boring into the back of my neck. Now he is moving again. His steps start slowly and then quicken up. But he doesn't turn towards the kills; he goes straight on and away to the left and a few moments later the crunching of his steps suddenly dies. The tiger has stopped abruptly. Just why it is impossible to tell, but I get a sudden warning that something is wrong.

It looks like impending mischief. That thought burns into my brain even though I am not as yet sure what went wrong. Neither Bali nor I had moved or made a sound so it is reasonable to suppose that the tiger has not either seen or heard us. That is what is worrying me. After such a bold approach almost right up to the kills, it seems as though the tiger had *expected* to find someone near them. If that is true it means trouble: a desperate tiger ready to wipe out if he can anything that stands in the way of his meal.

I want to warn Bali of the danger in case the silence tempts him to speak or move. But I dare not make the slightest sound or movement and can only hope he senses that all is not well. The minutes tick away. Each one of them seems like an hour as I wait with every nerve taut for something to happen.

Then, at first vaguely and without quite knowing why, I feel that the danger has passed. A few moments later, I know what told me. The fresh morning breeze which has sprung up from the east. Its gentle gusts are blowing in from behind us and bringing with them some disturbing sounds. The first ones had been faint, but now they are stronger and a sudden sickening wave of apprehension surges round my stomach. *Hell—surely not that?*

For a few moments I cannot trust my voice. Then I turn slowly round to Bali and ask in a whisper, '*When did you last see your brother?*'

His small head pokes round my arm and he hisses back that he last saw his brother Gopal running away through the stampeding herd. That answer does nothing to reassure me and I realize that my question has come too late; it should have been asked immediately I'd had that disturbing thought when Bali was chewing the bulls' eyes.

I listen again to the sounds coming in on the breeze and the sick feeling in my stomach rises. The message is only too plain. Not far away from us the tiger is feeding.

What a mess I've made of the whole business! By missing the one clue that really mattered—the two cowherds who didn't get home—I have driven a tiger to his first meal of human flesh. And I could have prevented it; for if the search had gone on after I had found Bali I should have found his brother, too. But instead of searching I had just sat on in the machan—and denied to the tiger throughout the night both the cow and the calf.

In such ways are man-eaters made. The first attack on a man nearly always is an accident. That probably is what has happened here, for if Bali's brother had got in the tiger's way the brute would have struck him down. To start with, however, the tiger would not have returned to the boy's body because to eat such a strange victim would not have occurred to him. Then, when he had been kept away from the cow and the calf, a gnawing hunger had at last reminded him that there had been a third kill as well. . .

■

All I can do now is to wait for daylight. My watch says that it is just five o'clock and the false dawn has already come and gone. As the ghastly sounds of feeding go on, a feverish anxiety is building up inside me. Time seems to be standing still as one thought tortures my mind: Will it be light enough to shoot by before the tiger makes off?

At last, the first glow of day tips the eastern horizon. Slowly the dim grey shapes of trees struggle out of the darkness; then colour comes seeping into their trunks and leaves. I wipe the dew off the rifle and check the action; when I glance along the barrel I can see the sights.

Not far from the foot of the machan tree, I find a game-path leading in the direction from which the sounds of feeding are still coming. Fifty yards along it, the jungle opens out into a grassy glade with scattered patches of bushes and clumps of saplings. At the fringe of the trees I check behind some cover. Although the tiger is now very close I still can't see him, but the noise he is making rivets my eyes on a patch of thorns out in the centre of the glade. The grisly meal is going on behind that.

The grass is sparkling with dew and my boots glide through it with only a faint swish. I am creeping off slowly to the left of the thorns and making for an isolated cluster of bushes. From there I can see a good line of approach which will bring me up under cover to within forty yards of the tiger.

I am nearly there. Conditions for stalking are ideal for the sodden grass is like a thick carpet and friendly bushes have shielded me every foot of the way. In front of me now are three clumps of bushes staggered in a line. Just to the right of the far one I can see the edge of the thorns. The tiger is still feeding and unsuspicious.

Slower now. I am taking every step with the greatest care for the first clump of bushes is behind me and I am making towards the second. When I'm up to it I pause to steady down and to take a final look at the rifle. Then, moving as slowly as I can, I start to edge round it. A moment later I have stopped.

The third clump of bushes is now only ten yards ahead and a lot more of the thorns have come into view. So has the tiger. He is about forty yards off, crouched in fairly high grass and tearing at something I can't see on the ground. He is facing towards me. If I move any farther out from the shelter of the bushes he must see me.

I don't move a muscle while two plans for taking the shot race round my head. All the time I have been staring hard at the tiger. That was a mistake. Telepathy must have warned him, for before I can make up my mind he springs up with a sudden *WOOF!* and stands looking straight at me.

The sight of a tiger over a fresh kill he has just gutted and started to eat is a sight you can never forget. The forelegs of this one were covered with blood and muck right up to his chest and his mask was stained a sickening red.

As I take a quick step away from the bushes the tiger's ears slap flat against his head and he crouches back.

I never knew what he was going to do. In the instant when he steadies after the crouch, the first bullet slams him to the grass with his legs kicking in the air. A moment later he's a snarling blur of threshing yellow fury as he tries to rise. He nearly makes it when he suddenly rears up on his hind quarters with his forepaws clawing frantically at the air. The second bullet takes him in the neck and crashes him back to the ground where he lies still.

I watch him carefully for more than a minute with the foresight steady on the white chest half hidden in the grass. The last shudder has run through his body and he seems to be dead. Even so I wait a little longer and then throw some sticks. One lands on him and he does not move.

Still keeping him covered I walk slowly towards him. He's dead—sprawled in a spreading pool of blood beside his third kill. As I look down at him the strain of the last few hours suddenly catches up and I flop to the grass and feel for a cigarette. When it's alight I call to Bali. He must be worried, but he'll be as relieved as I am to see that the thing in the grass beside the tiger is only another cow.

While I'm waiting for Bali to come up, I am thinking of the trouble and worry I might have saved myself during the night by keeping off all those wonderful theories.

EIGHT ANNAS A TAIL

It was six o'clock of a May morning and already unpleasantly warm. As Babs and I sipped our early tea under the shade of the trees near the house, we told each other quite unnecessarily that it was going to be another scorching day. Speaking for myself I did not really mind: the hot month of May is a slack one and I was going to spend the morning on a cool veranda with a new book; after lunch I might raise the energy to answer some letters.

Jumbo, one of the dogs, was feeling lazy too and lay stretched at my feet, a shaggy and rather oversized cocker spaniel. He had always hated the heat, and unless I took him down to the river to bathe he would not stir out until the cool of evening for he was a wise old man of twelve summers.

Those were our plans at six in the morning and for a hot day they were sound. Unfortunately, they did not last very long; for even as we made them, fate and the jungle were decreeing that our day should be very different indeed. For me it was to be a day that is still branded across my memory; for poor old Jumbo it was to mark the end of the road. . .

Bandarwallahs! Bandarwallahs! It was Kalu racing up through the orchards and shouting as he came. I knew at once what he was coming to tell me, another raid by the 'monkey-men' who had already visited us twice before. As soon as Kalu had caught up with his breath, I asked him where he had seen them. When he had told me I gulped down my tea and then went in to dress.

This time I was really going to catch them and discourage further visits; for these are cruel devils that come armed with nets, clumsy traps and old muzzle-loading guns. The live monkeys—and they prefer them to be very young—are for export and vivisection; the ones they cannot catch in their traps are shot down for the new government reward of eight annas a tail.

Now you might well imagine that as a farmer with large orchards, I should be only too happy to let these men go over the estate as often as they pleased. That, however, would be a wrong idea because by now I have the monkey situation pretty much under control whenever any fruits are on the trees. The monkeys, of course, always do some damage, but this is more than offset by the help these little animals give you about the jungles. Indeed, they might even save your life for they will often tell where a tiger or a leopard is hiding after a badly placed bullet.

Besides, the business of protecting the orchards developed long ago into an exciting game which I believe is enjoyed by the monkeys just as much as by us. I play it often for it takes me back to those early days when I was a senior member of the Black Hand and known over a wide-ish area as 'That bloody little horror with the catapult'. Now, alas, most of that puerile cunning with this weapon has gone, but some of the old magic of those times still returns when I pull back an elastic. But my own accuracy is no longer important as it is more than made up for by a little band of dusky 'sure-shots'—eager volunteers from the kids on the estate.

These young rustics know nothing of space suits and ray guns, and even cowboys and Indians are as yet unknown. They are thoroughly old-fashioned kids and so content with a simple 'catty' and a pocketful of smooth pebbles—and the red bottoms of the monkeys in the tree-tops. . .

That morning, as soon as I was dressed, I set off after the monkey-men with Jumbo at my heels. We walked fast for I was hoping to find them before they could do much damage. I was carrying a rifle while Jumbo had his old red and blue ball bulging from his mouth. Somewhere, he hoped, we should stop by water and play his favourite game.

I was making for a deep and shady nullah which runs diagonally through the estate and divides it into two almost equal halves. The banks of this are lined with magnificent trees, most of them tall stately kohas, which are loved by the monkeys for the cool shade of their topmost branches. So it was somewhere along here that I expected to find the monkey-men at work because this nullah is more than three miles long and the trees above it 'home' for at least six troops of monkeys.

The estate is roughly square, so I started the search at the far north-eastern corner and intended to stalk along the nullah until I found the raiders. By now the morning was really hot. There was little breeze and even under the shade of the trees the fierce heat from the sun was unpleasant. During the rains this nullah is a raging torrent, but now the flow of water had dried up leaving along the winding bed a series of crystal-clear pools with little fish darting above the pepper-and-salt of their sandy bottoms. By the side of most of these pools, at the foot of the high bank, are small ledges a foot or two wide and a few inches above the surface of the water. These are paths that have been beaten out by game and are much used at night by all kinds of animals. As the days grow warmer and the smaller pools elsewhere dry up, tigers and leopards begin to haunt the banks of this nullah.

For the first mile, I found no sign of the raiders. Then I picked up what were almost certainly their tracks: five pairs of human feet, the prints fresh and over the marks of the hooves and pads left by last night's visitors. At one spot these men had stopped to rest. The ground here was littered with *bidis*, the Indian leaf cigarette; and in one place against the bank some heavy bundles had been thrown down, one of them leaving on the sand a criss-crossed pattern like a net.

If those signs had not been enough to tell me that the monkey-men were not far ahead, the next pool two hundred yards down the nullah left no doubt of it. The grey bodies of two langur monkeys lay just by the water's edge. One was dead and nearly cold, the other still lived though its life was flowing rapidly away into a pool of blood seeping into the sand. Both bodies were peppered with red-brown spots where the shot that had brought them tumbling from the trees had slammed in. Neither of the monkeys had a tail.

I had known the troop from which these monkeys came for many years and had always regarded its little members as some of my best jungle friends. In many ways, this was the most useful troop of all along the whole stretch of the nullah. The ground here is tricky: beyond the banks it is covered with heavy forest and to the north rises steeply to several hundred feet. Towards the summit of this high ground are patches of open rocky scrub. These places are difficult to reach: the way up to them is over large boulders which have between them a mass of 'wait-a-bit' thorns and other rampageous weeds; these hide deep crevices so completely that a false step can mean a heavy fall; end up at the bottom of one of these with a broken limb and you might never be found.

All these high places are loved by leopards. They come up in the early morning to take the sun and stretch out on the flat-topped rocks. As the day gets warmer, they move to some shady spot to doze away the drowsy hours until night; but although they appear to sleep one eye is always cocked towards the nullah below. Long stretches of it are laid bare from these high places and anything moving on the sandy bed can be seen plainly. It is seldom that there is not a leopard somewhere about here, and whenever one of these sneaking brutes becomes a nuisance, this is the spot I come to first. Then it was that the monkeys used to help, for if a leopard was indeed about they would tell me—sooner or later—where it was.

As I looked up from the bodies of the two monkeys a cold anger took hold of me. The whole troop seemed to have been wiped out for there was no sign of the others anywhere. No swaying branches up in the trees as they swung from bough to bough, and in the air were none of their usual cries as they quarrelled and played above the pool. For the next fifteen minutes my anger mounted and there was but one thought in my mind: to catch these men, free whatever captives they had, and—but that could wait until I caught them.

That morning, however, I was not to catch them. Indeed, that satisfaction only came many years later when I surprised a big camp of them one morning just before dawn. But on that occasion I got them all: men, women and children, all their monkeys and all their goods and chattels. The chattels included the skins of buck, chital and barking deer, as well as an enormous bundle of peacock feathers. The skins and the feathers were a lucky find; for although those rascals had no licence to trap I could not have touched them for the monkeys alone.

All that, however, was still in the future and not known to me that morning when I set off after finding the dead monkeys to track their killers. In the sand I could see that two men had stayed in the nullah while the other three had probably worked the banks. At two places they had stopped to smoke again; then, at a spot where a game-path crosses the nullah, the footsteps of all five led away to the left and were lost on the harder surface of the track up on the bank. Now, I suspected, they were making for the river half a mile away where they would find a lot more monkeys.

I was about to go after them when I noticed that Jumbo was no longer at my heels. I whistled softly to bring him up from the pool in the nullah below. He was probably there wallowing like a buffalo with his beloved ball near his nose waiting for me to come and play. But there was no time for that now, so I sent down another and more urgent whistle when he did not come up to the first one.

I felt the first tinge of anxiety when a third call failed to bring him up. In a flash every other thought was swept from my mind and I raced back to the pool. Jumbo was not in sight, and when I started back the way I had come I saw none of his pug marks following mine. Now I was really worried. He was an obedient dog who without word to break would not have gone far on his own affairs.

From the pool I had just left to the one where we had found the two monkeys was just over a quarter of a mile with the nullah between them shaped like the letter S. Slowly I worked back scanning the sand for sign of Jumbo. But there was none, the soft surface showed only my own boots, the feet of the monkey-men and the tracks of wild animals.

There was still no trace of him when at last I was standing by the pool on the far side of which were the two monkeys. Across that placid surface was the last spot where I positively remembered Jumbo at my heels. So, from somewhere between where I stood now and the other end of the water—a distance of only eighty yards—that faithful old dog had vanished into thin air.

My eyes went to the little ledge running along by the water at the foot of the bank. A feeling of sick apprehension was churning inside me and every instinct was warning of what I should find when I went along that ledge.

For five minutes more I stood still and listened to the jungle. Nothing was excited; all the birds were going about their business in a calm way, and from nowhere around me came the slightest sign that anything was wrong. What I needed to tell me the truth was monkeys, but when I scanned the trees again there was still not one in sight. Slowly I started towards the ledge by the side of the pool.

Half-way along it I stopped. In the firm clay at my feet was the whole story and it told me that Jumbo was dead.

Almost at the water's edge was the single imprint of a leopard's paw. The pad had rammed hard into the clay with the toes wide-cleft and the claws straining out. A little to the left of the pug a small patch on the ledge had been swept clean of the debris and dead leaves fallen from the trees above. The leopard had sprung down from the bank, seized Jumbo by the neck, and then shaken him so violently that his body had swept that patch. And about a yard from the ledge, motionless and just showing above the surface of the pool, a spot of faded red and blue that was Jumbo's old ball.

Of the attack I had heard nothing, and why Jumbo had stayed so far behind me I shall never know. I can only think that he must have lingered about the bodies of the two monkeys and then, when he set out to follow me, he had picked up the leopard's scent. That would have stopped him, for he was well aware of the danger from these sneaking cats. By then I must have been round the first bend of the S in the nullah.

From the swept patch the leopard had gone on along the ledge carrying Jumbo with his legs trailing through the dead leaves by the water's edge. Then, a few yards beyond the pool, Jumbo—still alive—had broken the leopard's grip and shaken free. For a few glorious seconds, for he was a fighting man, he had kept the leopard off. The sand here had been wildly churned by both the leopard's pugs and Jumbo's in what had been a short but furious melee. Then sheer brute force had driven Jumbo back against the bank where he had been seized again. From here the leopard had gone on down the nullah and then had bounded up the bank towards that rocky and difficult ground.

I followed slowly, the trail made easy by frequent spots of blood. After climbing steeply for about fifteen minutes, I stopped. From a dense patch of scrub farther up the slope I had suddenly heard the leopard.

I am not going to try to describe my feelings. All I can say, passing over the agony, is that a burning fury was urging me on to rush forward and stop those dreadful sounds by any means. But I fought the urge back. To rush forward now would probably send the leopard flying from the back of the scrub and leave him free to operate another day. It might have been very unwise, too, and no help to Jumbo now, to rush straight at an unsuspecting leopard on a fresh kill. Patience was the only thing. If I held my hand and waited, I might get the revenge I wanted.

But not from here. When I had looked around me again I soon saw that I could get no nearer to the leopard without giving myself away. The ground was too difficult: the fifty or so yards I still had to climb before I stood the slightest chance were strewn with rocks and crackling leaves. The leopard had picked his spot with instinctive cunning and from no side could he be surprised; the only thing was to leave him where he was and then set a trap on ground of my own choosing.

The morning by now was so hot that there was one place the leopard was sure to come to when he had finished. That place was the pool immediately below me. When he came down to drink, as he must, I could kill him from the other side of the nullah.

With the greatest care I crept away from those heart-rending sounds, back down the rocks, then across the nullah and up the opposite bank where I found some cover to hide me.

The leopard took his time. It was over half an hour before I heard him moving boldly on the hill—an animal unsuspicious of any danger. About half-way down he started to roll in the dead leaves; then he spent some time cleaning his claws, tearing them through the bark of a tree with sharp, plucking little jerks. All at once I saw him weaving through the trees at the foot of the high ground across the nullah—a comparatively small animal as his pugs had shown. When he reached the bank above the pool he paused and looked to his right and left. A moment later he came down the bank in a gracefully controlled slide to stand on the ledge beside the water.

He gave me a beautiful broadside shot as he bent to drink with the points of his elbows sharp above his back. But I was a little too eager to see him dead and raised the rifle a shade too quickly. The leopard saw the movement from the corner of his eye. In a flash his head was up and looking straight towards me. As he braced for the spring that would take him away to safety I snatched at the trigger.

I heard the bullet strike and saw the leopard leap into the air. At the top of his jump he twisted and clawed for the bank. For one uncertain moment he hung there fighting for a hold with a blur of scrabbling paws. As I ripped back the bolt I thought he was going to drop; but with a sudden effort he was up and racing away through the trees. The bullet I sent after him hit a rock well behind his tail.

Although the first shot had been poorly placed he was nevertheless a badly wounded animal and that mad rush would not take him far. Or so I thought, but when I went to look for him I sought in vain for over an hour. There was no sign of him anywhere about the spot where I thought he should have fallen; nor on the high ground was there any trace of his passing; and nowhere was there a single drop of blood. At last I came to the conclusion that I must have left him somewhere behind me and so decided to go back to the beginning—the claw marks at the top of the nullah bank.

From here, as I had seen before, his first wild rush had taken him about a hundred yards. Then all trace of him was lost as the ground began to rise and became rocky. I started to search around the end of this trail again, and I had only been going for about a minute when I suddenly found a clue. Across the side of a rock was a heavy smear of blood. As I bent down to examine it I was wondering how I could have missed it the first time.

But had I missed it? The rock had been catching the full rays of the sun for some time and was burning hot when I touched it. Now my follow-up had started more than an hour before, yet this blood was still wet and just beginning to trickle down the rock. *I've walked right into it!* As the thought hit me I froze beside the rock: the leopard had been here within the last few minutes and now was probably watching me from somewhere close by.

Any sudden movement now might bring the enraged beast on top of me. He might come even if I did not move, but it was safer to stay crouched by the rock and let my eyes search as far as they could from under the brim of my hat. There was no sign of him in front of me, so fervently hoping that he was not somewhere close behind I started slowly to my feet. A few breathless moments later; after I had looked all round, the tension slackened. The sudden rush would have come before now if the leopard had been really near.

It had been a nasty scare and I now started off much more cautiously. Not far from the blood-smeared rock a game-path led towards the nullah. That was the way I thought the leopard would have gone. The heat now was like a furnace and a burning thirst had probably driven him back to the pool. I was, however, taking no more chances; for it was just as possible that he had moved on from the rock because he had heard me coming and might now be waiting in ambush somewhere ahead.

As I moved slowly towards the pool, I found more blood on the path. This certainly was the way he had gone and I doubled my precautions. Every bit of cover likely to conceal a leopard was now suspect indeed and had to be scrutinized carefully before going on. After I had stalked forward for another hundred yards the ground in front of me rose in a gentle fold before it rolled down to the nullah on the other side. If the leopard was planning mischief, just over the crest of that was a likely place for him to spring it.

A little before the fold started to rise I left the game-path and went thirty yards to the right of it. From this new position, I began to creep up the slope as carefully as I could. At the top of it I paused with my finger on the trigger and my eyes everywhere at once. Suddenly I knew that the leopard was not here. Of that I was perfectly sure, for on one of the topmost branches of a *koha* tree almost above my head was a monkey.

From where it sat, it could take in a sizeable piece of the surrounding jungle. Yet it was calm and quiet, and from the ground appeared to be dozing. That told me that no leopard was or recently had been anywhere near here; for if that monkey had caught even a glimpse of its spotted hide it would now be racing round the tree and screaming in high alarm.

With the tension suddenly slackened and the leopard heaven knew where, I fished out a pipe. Why, I wondered as I filled it, had the leopard so abruptly changed his mind and avoided the nullah? The most probable answer was that he had either seen or heard me close behind him and had realized the danger of going down to the pool. If that was true, then he had for a certainty doubled back to the high ground. One thing, however, was sure: the leopard knew where I was and so it would be unwise to go back from my present position. The safest thing was to let him think I had lost his trail by going on to the nullah. Then, once I was by the pool and out of sight, I could fool him by working round to the high ground from behind.

As I started towards the path leading down to the pool, I was thinking again of Jumbo. Once more, I was living through the agony of hearing the leopard at his meal. So it happened that as I reached the path the memory of that ordeal was undoubtedly dulling my mind and in some odd way splitting it into two differently thinking parts. I was half-way down the path when I came abruptly into the deep shadow cast by the trees along the bank. Just beyond this and straight ahead of me was a patch of blinding sunlight and the dazzling reflection from the pool. The two together were so bright that for a moment I closed my eyes.

When I opened them again, it seemed that one part of my mind showed me the spotted back of a leopard crouched half behind the root of a tree and a small bush on the path six feet ahead. At the same time, the other part of my mind was assuring me that no leopard could be there while a monkey sat silent overhead. A little confused but nevertheless sure that this could not be a leopard, I walked on expecting to see that spotted back resolve into the litter of dead leaves it had to be.

It was only one pace short of the bush that my confusion vanished when the full length of the leopard leapt into view. For a second that seemed eternity, I looked down at him. Neither of us moved and for one brief moment I thought he was dead. But he was alive, and an instant later, with a snarl of rage, he reared up in a blur of flailing paws. I tried to leap clear and went crashing into the bank. As I fought to keep my balance, sharp claws raked down my left leg. I raised my foot to kick them off and the leopard's jaws snapped shut round the heel of my boot. I slammed it down with his head still clamped to it. But with my foot caught tight, I lost the last of my balance and fell heavily to the path.

Now he had me. A quick spring and the game was his. But he did not move. He might have been dead except for his furious eyes screaming hate into mine. I knew then that he was at his last gasp, but even though his strength was failing fast, I could feel his jaws straining tighter round my boot. By now I had found and grabbed up the rifle. The next second I jammed the muzzle into his mouth and pulled the trigger.

He died at once. But although I had felt the blast through my boot, it was some little time before I had prised his fangs from the rubber heel. Reaction hit me as soon as my foot was free. I was trembling with shock and my heart was pounding at top speed while the deep claw marks down my leg were streaming blood. I should have liked to lie down beside the dead leopard, but before I could move a wild scream of terror ripped through the air. It came so abruptly and held such a chilling note that I was on my feet in a flash and grabbing for the rifle expecting I knew not what.

All at once I remembered the monkey. It had to be that for the scream had come from high above me. From where I was I could not see it through the leaves of the trees, but the scream had startled me so much that I began to run towards the top of the bank. Just as I reached it and was looking up the scream came again and stopped me in utter amazement.

What sort of monkey was this? It didn't call at leopards and seemed so bad at climbing trees that it was about to fall off the one it was on; for it was hanging from a branch with its arms at full stretch and kicking its legs feebly in the air. Without warning, the scream rent the air again. Then before my startled eyes the monkey let go its hold. It dropped like a stone, a sudden twisting flash of grey that hurtled down thumping from branch to branch until it hit the ground with a sickening thud sixty feet below.

I was still surprised, but as I made my way down to it an idea was forming in my mind. The monkey had fallen by the water's edge with its face upwards and one quick look was enough to tell me why it had not called at the leopard and why it had fallen off the tree. It was a young male monkey and it had been dying for hours. Its body was peppered with the shot from a muzzle-loading gun and it had been blinded in both eyes. It would have fallen from the tree in any case, but I believe that the sudden report of my shot at the leopard had so terrified it anew that it slipped from its perch; then, weak from loss of blood and hanging over a sixty-foot drop in a strange and frightening world of blackness and pain—well, who wouldn't scream?

At last I slung the rifle and started to limp up the slope towards home. As I stepped out a whistle instinctively formed on my lips to call up Jumbo before I remembered. At the top of the slope I paused and looked down at the dead monkey. Its little face seemed slightly ashamed and saying, 'I couldn't really help it, you know.'

THE LAUGHING LEOPARD

Three years ago I would have said that there was no such thing as a leopard with a sense of humour. And with good cause; for up to that time these pests had claimed four of our dogs and innumerable livestock and so I had hunted them with little mercy ever since we came here. In seven years there had been many encounters, but in none of them had I found in the leopard's make-up anything more than meanness and a cunning that made them really dangerous when wounded. Indeed, any animal less given to smiling than these overgrown cats would have been difficult to imagine.

It was in 1955 that the humorist, which eventually became known to us as the Muskiata Leopard, changed my mind. It was all very annoying, for on the first evening we met this leopard certainly made a fool of me and undoubtedly left smiling broadly. I tried for him again, but once more he got away and by early the next morning was not only smiling but chuckling loudly. After the third try it was worse; as I walked back from that I could imagine his deep belly-laughs rolling round the jungle.

In three frustrating days the leopard took every trick. He was far too cunning, and by the evening of the third day I admitted defeat and started for home. It was then that he sneaked up for the biggest laugh of all and got away with an act so bold and cock-a-snook that at first I did not believe it. But there was no doubt about the blood on the sand and an old and willing friend lay dead. After that, a cold anger sent me back to the village determined to kill the laughing leopard.

He came again the next night. But when he crossed the starlit sand of the riverbed he was no longer laughing for the thing he wanted least of all had at last arrived. . .

I had been hearing about this leopard for several days before I finally went to meet him. By all accounts he was an unmitigated nuisance of the first water. Goats were his main target, but he was taking so many that he was obviously killing for the sheer joy of it. When he was not on goats, he was harrying cattle.

At first I did nothing about it for the killings were going on some eight miles from the estate. Mischievous leopards were nothing new and just then I was busy spraying fruit trees. Then the two men arrived with the litter. In it was a small and frightened boy with a bloodstained bandage round his head and another round his left leg.

I left home an hour later. Twenty minutes before that, one of our bullock-carts loaded with camp stores had gone ahead with Bhutu—my best shikari—driving. I caught it up at the Denwa River, in time to be ferried across the shallow stream meandering down the wide sandy bed. When I was settled in the cart, I asked Bhutu what he thought we should find. He shrugged his shoulders: 'Who can tell with a leopard? It might have been playing or just frightened. But if it has turned into a bad one we shall have trouble; that kind hunts only by night. But let us see what they have to say in the village—we are nearly there . . .'

■

The boy had been attacked in a wide sandy nullah strewn with rocks. He had gone there that morning with his father to help water a flock of goats. It had all happened very quickly, but the boy's father was sure that the attack had been deliberate and the general opinion now was that this leopard had turned man-eater and would soon strike again. He was still on the outskirts of the village, and shortly before our arrival had been heard calling.

Nobody was really keen to take us right up to the nullah where the attack had taken place. That was understandable; jungle men fear the leopard perhaps more than any other animal for they know that even a well-armed man is not always safe from the speed and cunning of its attack. In the end, a small party of men led us out some half-mile from the village and then one of them pointed to a line of trees ahead: 'The nullah runs between those.'

We found the pool where the goats had watered in the morning by the countless tracks scarring the sand. There was also something else to tell us that we had found the right place: lying near some rocks about fifty yards away was a long strip of grubby white cloth. It was the boy's turban, and near it were the blurred impressions left by the dancing paws of a big male leopard. Ten yards from these, behind a cluster of rocks nestling in coarse grass, was a smooth depression in the sand; the spot where the brute had lain hidden before the attack.

Bhutu was shaking his head: 'This is a bad one all right. With a big flock of goats only fifty yards away, he chooses the boy.'

The pug marks went bounding across the sand to the

opposite side of the nullah. I followed them over and saw that the leopard had jumped to the grassy bank near a big rock. After that I lost them: under the grass the earth was baked hard and the soft paws had not marked it.

'See here, sahib!' Bhutu's sharp exclamation spun me round. He was a few yards from the big rock and peering down at something in the sand. I jumped back to the nullah and ran to join him.

Bhutu was pointing to a patch of wet sand which showed that the leopard had sprung back to the nullah from the bank I had just been exploring. But the leopard now was no longer alone; not far from his pug marks were the smaller tracks of a female. She had been crouching behind the big rock watching the attack on the boy. Here was the answer to that and to the recent spate of kills: what we had to deal with was no man-eater but more simply a lovesick 'show-off' leopard.

After the boy had been mauled, the happy couple had padded away down the nullah. We set off to follow their tracks and after a quarter of a mile came to a spot where shady trees clustered thickly along one back. The ground behind them was well wooded and rocky and rose sharply to some two hundred feet.

'This is where you will catch him,' whispered Bhutu.

The sand under the trees showed many 'scratch-marks' and in several places it was wildly churned up. Bhutu was right: somewhere on the high ground the leopards must have a snug retreat.

'Leave me your axe', I said, 'and then go back and bargain for the biggest billy goat in the village.'

When he had gone I climbed the bank opposite the high ground, went in a little way, and then started to cut thorns. I was going to tie the goat under the trees in the nullah and then watch it from a 'hide' I was just about to make among some rocks twenty yards away. Even now I can remember what I was thinking as I wielded the axe. It was going to be easy after all: by tomorrow morning the leopard's skin would be hanging out to dry.

The hide was nearly finished when I heard Bhutu coming back down the nullah. In a few minutes he appeared, sweating profusely and swearing hard as he dragged a villainous-looking goat behind him. 'This shaitan', he grumbled loudly, 'is so angry and strong that he will probably kill the leopard.'

Between us we got the goat under the trees and tied it to a root. Then, after we had finished the hide, I missed my bag of cartridges. If I had been carrying a rifle with a full magazine it would not have mattered; but I had brought a shot-gun, and against two leopards in the dark I might well need more ammunition than the two rounds of buckshot in the chambers. I had a vague idea that I had put the bag down by the big rock. But I was not sure, and so Bhutu would have to look for it there while I went back to where I had cut the thorns.

In fifteen minutes I was back after a thorough search had failed to find it. As I jumped back to the nullah, I noticed that the goat was lying down. From a few paces off it seemed to be asleep, but when I got up to it I saw that its eyes were wide open. The next moment it jerked up its head, took two deep breaths—and died. Then I saw the deep punctures in its neck and the pug marks of the leopard in the sand.

It was futile to go after him. But thoroughly annoyed with myself for tossing him such an easy chance, I climbed the bank and looked round the jungle. The leopard was probably still near and quite likely watching me, but to imagine that he would show a hair of his hide was pure wishful thinking. I gave it up when I heard Bhutu scrunching back on the sand below me.

'Have a look at your "strong and angry" goat,' I said to him as he came up. He had found my bag; but now, with the leopard as much in our plans as we were, it seemed unlikely that I should need even one of the cartridges in the gun.

But with a show-off leopard almost anything can happen. This one might yet stick his neck out just a little too far. It was now nearly dark, and if Bhutu worked the usual trick of making enough noise for two men going off, the leopard might be fooled. A few minutes later, I was settled in the hide and Bhutu was talking loudly to himself as he walked home along the nullah.

It turned out to be one of the most uncomfortable and disturbed nights I have spent in the jungle. Several times I heard the leopards close by. But not once did I see them, nor did either of them come near the dead goat. Perhaps love had dulled their appetites, but it seemed to me that they were perfectly well aware of my presence in the hide. That thought kept me on edge the whole night, for with only a thin screen of thorns, I felt like a mouse in a flimsy trap waiting the cat's pleasure. Just before dawn they cleared off for the last time and a little later the leopard 'sawed' from the high ground behind me.

It had been a freezing night, and when I crawled from the hide at sun-up I was cramped and shivering. For several minutes I stamped about the sand to restore my circulation; then, at a fast pace, I made for camp where I found Bhutu crouched over a roaring fire boiling a kettle. A few minutes later I was drinking a steaming cup of tea. When I had had a second one I was going back to wipe that satisfied smile from the leopard's face.

The stalk that had been so impossible the night before might now succeed. For a start I knew roughly where the leopards were: on top of that high ground. Secondly, they had had an exciting night, and both of them by now were probably fast asleep. And because it was still cold and they were sun-loving creatures, the odds said that they would be lying on rocks in the open. All I had to do was to find them. . .

Three hours later, I had given it up. Along the whole length of the narrow crest of the high ground and on the slopes each side of it there had not been a sign of them. Tired and hot, I started slowly down the steep slope to the nullah below. Before going back to camp I intended to cover up the dead goat to hide it from vultures. It might yet bring the leopards back; for when they woke up they would certainly be hungry and then they would remember the meal they had passed up last night. By that time I should be back in the hide.

The goat was not there. At least not much of it, for all I found was a mess on the sand and the remains of one foreleg still held by the rope. The lovers had snatched their meal while I was looking for them on the hill. It was then that I thought I heard the leopard chuckle.

The only thing to do now was to start again. In his present mood, the leopard would take another goat at once even though he was not hungry. But I should have to start sitting early and hope that he came by daylight; from a 'show-off' kill he might be gone in a few seconds.

By three o'clock in the afternoon everything was ready. This time I was sitting on a well-hidden machan in a tree overlooking a fresh goat on the sand below. And in case the leopard was suspicious of this goat, four others had been tied at different places along the nullah to give me another chance tomorrow night.

The afternoon dragged by without a sign of him. Then, as evening deepened into night, there was a false alarm which kept me tensed up for an hour after peafowl had screamed from the undergrowth close by. By the time it seemed safe to relax from that, the stretch of sand beneath me was in black shadow.

Half an hour later the leopard came. A sudden sharp tinkle from the goat's bell was the only warning. A second after that the goat was dead. All that had marked its passing was a slight scuffle and a choking gasp; the whole performance might have taken five seconds. For the rest of that night I stayed ready to meet him if he sneaked back to feed. He did not come, and to say that I was surprised would not be true. Why, after all, should he come? He was still bursting with the goat he had eaten in the morning.

Soon after dawn I climbed down to the sand and, with a piece of rope from the machan over a branch, I hauled the dead goat up until it was well above my head. The leopard could whistle for this one until I was ready. When I got back to camp I sent Bhutu off for the other four goats; then I had breakfast and turned in. Bhutu woke me about an hour later.

'What is it?' I asked him.

'All the goats are dead.'

The leopard had made quite a night of it. Five goats in a row and he had not eaten from one of them. However, I was too tired then to wonder about the next move; that would be something to think about when I got up for tea.

It certainly was, although the problem of what to do now was an easy one. Just go home. To waste more time would be foolish, for even as I slept the leopard had made the situation worse by snatching two more goats from the village flock. This Romeo did not seem to sleep at all; he was everywhere at once and all the time and to go on trying for him could only result in another heap of dead goats.

My plans had been based on just one kill, but the leopard now had seven choices for his evening meal. There were five goats scattered along the nullah, two somewhere else from the village flock, and heaven alone knew how many other kills he might have hidden in the jungle as well. Where he would feed tonight was anybody's guess. So let him be. The best course was to go quietly home and remember the laughing leopard as just one of those things. . .

■

By the time Bhutu and I had had something to eat and struck camp, it was dark. That, however, did not worry us for there were only eight miles to go and it was a fine starlit night; by ten o'clock we ought to be home. As soon as the cart had creaked out of the village, Bhutu drew a blanket over his head and settled down to sleep. I lit a pipe, leaned back in my chair and prepared to enjoy the leisurely ride under the stars. The bullocks could safely be left to themselves: there was only one track and they would plod stolidly on until something stopped them.

A mile from the village the track starts dipping down to cross the sandy bed of the Denwa River. As we neared this, I leaned forward to listen to the jungle. All about here was the area the leopards were working, the nullah they lived in joining the river two hundred yards upstream from the track. But the night was still and peaceful, the leopard probably was already dining his mate on one of his many kills.

I settle back in my chair and soon hear the hard crunch of the iron tyres on the track give way to a soft purr as we reach the sandy bed of the river. It really is a beautiful night, cool and crisp with only the light from the stars. I am leaning back and staring up at them when the right-hand bullock stumbles heavily. The cart stops with a jerk which fetches me upright. The bullock has fallen down and is lying on the sand; his team-mate is straining to break away from the yoke. I prod Bhutu with my foot: 'Hey! Raja has fallen asleep. Shake him up.'

Bhutu's tousled head appears from under the blanket. He sees the bullock lying down and reaches forward sleepily to twist its tail. The bullock does not move and Bhutu starts muttering rude things about its ancestors as he gets out of the cart. I watch him go round to the bullock's head where he tries to get it to its feet with a jerk on its nose string. Still the bullock stays down and I see Bhutu drop to his knees on the sand. A moment later he looks up: 'The bullock is dead, sahib—and the sand is covered with blood.'

For a moment I think he is joking, but I get out of the cart and switch on the torch. The sand under the bullock's head is wet and red, and when I bend down I see what has happened. In a lightning rush from below, the leopard has torn its throat out.

Six goats and now a willing old bullock. As I look down at it, I am conscious of being angry yet at the same time I can see the humour of the situation the leopard has left us in. I can also imagine him somewhere up on the bank laughing himself sick and saying to his sweetheart, 'I do hope you were watching, my dear. Even when they're that size they don't scare *me!*'

All at once that vision of the leopard gave me the idea I should have thought of before. By now I was in any case going back to kill him no matter how many goats I had to feed to him first. But this new idea did not call for a single goat and it would not matter a scrap if the leopard had a hundred kills littered about the jungle. Yet the idea was simple: tomorrow night I was going to pit this spotted humorist against the one thing he really did not want around . . . another leopard.

There was nothing difficult about that and early the next morning I called one of the village tanners and a potter. Two hours later they had what I wanted ready. Then Bhutu and I spent several hours on the riverbed digging a pit in the sand some twenty yards beyond the dead bullock.

■

It is just six o'clock and the evening light is fading. We have been in the pit for five minutes where Bhutu had settled himself a little behind me. His role is that of an eager, challenging male leopard while my job—if the opposition comes—is not only to stop it before it can get too close, but to watch out for the leopardess who will not be above trying to have a look at the new boyfriend. Across my knee is the best weapon I know for a close quarter set-up that might become lively—the 12-bore loaded with buckshot.

In a whisper I ask Bhutu if he is ready. He grins and tightens the short length of knotted cord smeared with bees-wax. Then he jams the 'leopard' we had had made in the morning firmly between his knees. I make a last quick check of the shotgun and torch and then nod my head.

HAW-a-HAW-a-HAW-a-HAW-a-HAW! The deep 'sawing' of a leopard rolls across the sands and goes echoing round the hills.

We are answered immediately by a suddenly scared troop

of langur monkeys in the koha trees across the river. *Ca! Cha! Whoop-a-Whoop-a-WHOOP!* As their cry goes up, peafowl in the trees farther down join in with their cat-like *Mee-eeow! Mee-EEOW!*

Soon the whole jungle is alive with alarms. Unconscious allies all, for every warning cry is guaranteeing Bhutu as a genuine leopard. At intervals for the next half-hour, he keeps calling. The jungle keeps excited, but about the only thing that has not answered us yet is the leopard. But that may be a good sign. If he is coming——

'*There he is!*' Bhutu's hoarse whisper and pointing finger puts me on him at once. He has just come down the river bank about a hundred yards away. As he reaches the white sand, he becomes harder to see for the last of the light has nearly gone. But I can still see him as he creeps along the sand with his belly pressed close against it. He is almost up to the bullock when he stops and my hands tighten on the gun. Suddenly he springs—straight on top of the bullock. He is crouched low and ready for instant action as his eyes search all round for his enemy.

A second later I have him in a narrow circle of brilliant light. A touch on the left trigger sends the buckshot whistling across in a tight pattern. As the pellets smash home behind his shoulder, he seems to freeze. But only for a moment; then it is like a picture in slow motion as his back arches and he draws slowly back dragging his front paws. We hear the claws ripping through the bullock's hide. The second barrel springs him high in the air and then sends him sprawling in a cloud of sand.

I reload quickly and start to sweep the light all around us. There is no sign of the leopardess. Which is just as well, for we want nothing to do with disappointed females tonight.

THE KHARNTA TIGER

'This has roared near the village every night since. He seems angry with us and we are all very frightened.'

It was three o'clock in the afternoon of a day towards the end of January. Squatting on the edge of our veranda was an old man who had just walked eight miles from his village to give me the first news of the Kharnta Tiger. It was a curious story. A tiger had suddenly turned dangerous immediately after a strange noise had disturbed it over a kill at night. What had made the noise nobody yet knew, but in a single second it had turned a tiger that had never given trouble before into a terrible menace.

The story had started after a party of woodcutters found a dead sambur hidden in thick jungle near the village. It was clearly a tiger's kill, for not only were there fang marks in the victim's neck, but on the sandy bed of a ravine near by the pug marks of the killer were plain. After finding it the party had moved on quickly; it was past six o'clock and a likely time for the tiger to come back for a feed.

The sambur lay about a hundred and fifty yards from the nearest of their scattered huts. That night the moon rose early, so when the tiger was heard to leave the hills some way to the west and start towards the kill, several men left the village and crossed a field to a thorn hedge fifty yards nearer to the jungle. The direction the tiger was coming from would take him over open ground before he reached the trees and the men were hoping to see him.

They waited by the hedge for nearly an hour, but when at the end of this time the tiger had not shown up, they started to drift back. The night had got chilly and with nothing to see, the best place was bed. As they came away all of them believed that the tiger had not yet arrived.

They were wrong. By the time the last man left, the tiger had probably been on the kill for fifteen minutes and had started to feed. Then something happened. Just what, no one yet knew, but one of the men from the village told me later that before all hell broke loose there was a sound 'like a stick striking the trunk of a tree'. This was followed a second later by a shattering roar. Then the tiger went mad. The same man telling of the appalling row that now arose described it as 'a furious forest devil beating the underbrush with a big tree'.

The uproar had lasted twenty minutes. Then the tiger had left the jungle and started to circle through the scrub about the village. He was still very angry, and to the frightened people huddled behind locked doors he seemed to be searching for the thing he had obviously failed to find near the kill.

The next morning a visit to the remains of the sambur showed the men a wide area of devastation all round it. Bushes had been flattened, several saplings were found bitten through, and the bark on nearly a dozen trees had been stripped by furious claws and teeth. But what had caused the tiger's sudden rage was still a mystery. There was no sign of anything that explained it, and even with their lifelong experience of the jungles, none of the men could say what had caused that strange noise the night before.

It was never heard again. But for the next few nights, the tiger came back and roared through the jungles around the village. Now, however, the men were hearing another sound as well whenever the brute passed particularly close to their huts. Some of them described it as a low moaning while others declared it was more like a snarled sigh of anger.

The real trouble started about a week after. The cattle had left the mangers soon after seven and an hour later were grazing along the bank of a wooded nullah half a mile away. The tiger came without warning for none of the cattle winded him creeping along the nullah bed. When he suddenly broke cover by a small bush on the bank, he was within a few yards of the nearest cow. It was a savage and vicious attack: the final toll was that first cow dead on the spot and three other animals so badly mauled that two of them died before evening.

When the last of the terrified herd had thundered out of sight, the tiger went back to the dead cow and dragged it to a small ravine a hundred yards away. There and then, he devoured nearly half of it. But he never returned for another feed, and during the whole time his career lasted, he was never known to visit a kill twice. . .

By the time the old man had finished his story, certain ideas had formed in my mind. Here was a very angry tiger which had suddenly taken to killing cattle. He was a very suspicious tiger, too, for he took his meals as soon as he had killed them and never returned for a second feed. Now the most likely thing to have caused both the sudden change and the suspicion was a bullet.

When I voiced this thought to the old man, he laughed.

'That is not possible here, huzoor,' he said. 'I will, of course, grant you that there are in our village several badmashes—men ready to do anything for a few annas and who would dearly love to get a tiger skin to trade. But none of us owns a gun and it is never possible to borrow one. Besides, if a shot had been fired that night, all of us would have heard it. . .'

■

Two days later, I saw this tiger's pug marks. I had gone over only for the morning because just then work would keep me at home for another five days. The pugs, which I first picked up in the powdery dust of a footpath, were certainly impressive; if the rest of the tiger was in proportion to these he must be one of the best specimens about. Just then, however, I was not concerned with his size. What intrigued me far more was the clue left by his pug marks, for it bore out the very thing I suspected. This tiger was walking with a great deal of his weight thrown on his right front paw. That surely meant some painful injury—probably around his left shoulder—and if my guess was right it had been inflicted by a bullet.

Once I was satisfied about that, I started home. What I had just read in the dust did not really surprise me and there was after all no mystery; in the old man's village someone *did* own a gun and it had probably been denied for the obvious reason: an unlicensed weapon. It would be an old muzzle-loader, and when it had been fired at the tiger it would have been double-shotted with two irregular lumps of lead. However, when charged with the crude 'country' powder, these weapons have poor penetration; but they inflict nasty wounds, and if the tiger had collected those two shots in his shoulder, they would certainly account for his crippled condition. If the wound healed well he would keep on cattle, but if it got worse hunger would force him to seek some easier prey.

To forestall that trouble if I could, it had been my intention to return in five days to start tying out live baits. However, on the morning of the fourth day after I had found the pug marks, the worst possible news came in. The tiger, by now, had moved over to another village some four miles nearer to the estate; and from there, two days before, a man had disappeared.

He had been in charge of the village cattle and had left with them in the morning. The first sign that anything was wrong came in the middle of the afternoon when some of the animals straggled back. That was unusual, though nobody at the time thought much of it. Then, late in the evening, the village became alarmed. All the animals were home but the cowherd was not. A search that evening and all the next day failed to find any trace of him. Not a scrap of clothing, not a shred of flesh, not a splinter of bone did anyone discover. The cowherd had vanished into thin air.

That altered the whole situation. The jungle man is pretty much of a fatalist whenever a tiger starts killing his cattle and he seldom makes any real effort to stop it. What actually would be the use? Something has happened to displease the Gods and he must just grin and bear it until their anger has passed. Cowherds, however, are a very different matter, and when a tiger starts killing them the jungle man sits up and takes some real notice.

The bad news travelled fast. In no time at all, and over a wide area, parties of men armed with spears and axes were going out with the cattle. The herds now no longer grazed through the jungles but were bunched together on open grasslands and kept well clear of any cover that might hide a tiger. Both men and cattle were now difficult to get at.

Wise precautions? On the evidence so far they were wise under one condition only, and that condition was that this tiger went right away, for if he stayed there was an alarming possibility. Nobody, of course, was yet sure about the fate of the missing cowherd, but if this tiger had killed him then it knew what an easy prey man was. That, to a desperately hungry tiger, would start a train of thought: Why bother with the herds and the armed men guarding them? Why not turn instead to the outskirts of villages and lonely forest paths? Places where there were unsuspecting people . . . drawing water . . . tending fields . . . bringing home supplies. . .

■

Five days passed without any kills, and I had begun to think that the tiger had moved away. Then, within the space of a few hours, more news about him came in. He had been seen three times moving very slowly, and there were two reports of herds suddenly restless for no apparent reason. That news was both good and bad. Good because no other attempt had been made to take a man and the restless herds suggested that the tiger was still trying to get at them. But to find that he had not gone away was bad, for by all the rules he should have made off because no tiger ever stays where there is nothing to eat. *But could he go away?* My guess was no, his wound now was too painful to let him move far.

The last time the tiger had been seen was at a spot some four miles from the estate. That was near enough to start tying out baits. For this tiger, however, there would be one unusual departure from normal practice: the baits would be tied during the day and not at night because he never came back for a second feed. And once they were out they would have to be watched carefully, for if one was taken that would be the time to try for this tiger in the only way that at present seemed to offer a chance—a stalk up to a fresh kill.

By eleven o'clock the next morning, eight baits had been rounded up and were waiting to be tied out at likely spots about our jungles. By mid-afternoon they had all been sited except one. Then, just as we were tying it, two breathless men came racing across from Tendukhera to say that less than twenty minutes before, the tiger had charged into their herd of cattle. It looked like the very opportunity I was now working for. Tendukhera is a small village only half a mile across the river, and if the tiger had killed, there was still plenty of time to catch him over the victim.

However, it was nearly an hour before we were sure of what had happened. After the charge there had been a great deal of confusion and while some of the cattle had bolted home, others had scattered about the jungle. No one knew whether the tiger had killed or not and the scene of the attack proved nothing: there was neither a dead animal nor any sign that one had been dragged away.

When the last cow had been rounded up and brought home, it was five-fifteen. None of the herd was missing; but down the right back leg of a small bullock were four long gashes still dripping blood which had been made by the claws of a tiger. As I looked at those four marks on a living animal, I knew that cattle were now more than this tiger could manage. He could maul but not kill—and that was not going to satisfy his hunger.

After seeing that bullock, I stood thinking for several minutes. There was no doubt now that this tiger's wound had got worse and he was not only badly crippled but also very hungry; it was likely, too, that he had been weakened still more by his recent attack on the herd. Would he have gone far after missing that bullock? It seemed to me that the answer was no, and what I thought more probable was that he was still somewhere close by—very angry and almost certainly planning what to do next about his gnawing hunger.

In that hunger lay the chance. It was the difference between a normal tiger and one which has started to prey on man. To get up to the first kind on foot you need lots of luck and all the skill you have; to find the second kind you need neither luck nor skill because if you make enough noise, he will find you.

There were nearly two hours of daylight left, and I decided to start from the scene of the attack. When I got there again I had another look all round but there still seemed to be nothing I had missed the first time; there was not even an indication to show in which direction the tiger had gone. However, one of the cowherds had been sure that he had made off to the south. Although it was not wise to bank too much on that because all of them had been very excited, it was nevertheless a likely direction. That way and not far off lay the foothills of the Satpura Mountains—and plenty of snug places to lie up in.

All afternoon a light breeze had been blowing steadily from the west. That was something I could now use; for if it kept steady the danger of a sudden rush could be confined to one side—the side away from the wind. In case that suggests that a tiger hunts by scent, let me add that he does nothing of the sort. He hunts entirely by sight and hearing, but as he learnt at his mother's knee that nearly every animal he preys on has a keen sense of smell, he always stalks *into* the wind. Even against man—for he just does not know that man's nose is no better than his own.

When I had left the scene of the attack some three hundred yards behind me, a small ravine barred my way. It was about twelve feet wide and six feet deep with a sandy bed. As I reached the bank, the first thing I saw was the tiger's tracks in the sand below me. On that loose surface his pug marks were indistinct but clear enough for me to make out that he was going mainly on three legs.

The tracks led up the ravine to the left and, keeping to the top of the bank, I started to follow them. After eighty yards, I came to a small pool which had a ring of mud all round it. From where I stood on the bank, I could see that the tiger had stopped to drink and had left some clean-cut impressions behind him. Then I looked at the water in the pool: it was still and clear and without a trace of muddy sediment clouding it. The water could not lie and it told me that the tiger had been gone some time.

I badly wanted a closer look at those pug marks, but before venturing down I set off to make a wide circle round the pool. When I was back to where I started I stood for another ten minutes listening; there was still no alarm of any kind and so I went down to the ravine and stood beside the pool. In the firm mud, the pug marks were perfect. At four places both the tiger's forepaws had been down together side by side. For a few moments I stared down at them not at all sure that my eyes were not playing me some trick. *What on earth was this?* As I bent down to examine them I was still not believing what I saw.

Monstrous! Now there was no getting away from it, for I was down on my knees and staring at the pug marks a foot away from my eyes. It was the impressions made by the left forepaw that riveted my attention and I went over all of them with the minutest care. When, at last, I stood up the whole picture of this tiger had changed and my theory of a bullet wound in the shoulder had been shattered.

As I stood by the pool filling a pipe, I began to fit the pieces of the story into place. They fell together easily, and by the time my pipe was alight I knew what had happened that first night and I knew too what had caused that sound like a stick striking the trunk of a tree. Just a thorn. And now it was in the pad of the tiger's left forepaw which was swollen to three times the size of the right one. In the deep depressions left by this pad I had seen the butt-end of it in all the impressions: a small irregular dot in the mud.

Just how the thorn got there I can picture clearly. I can see the tiger on that first night moving above the dead sambur and tearing at the flesh. On the ground near by is a dead branch fallen from one of the many jungle thorn trees. The thorns on this, perhaps two inches or more long, are brittle and ready to snap off. All at once that incautious paw finds one and the sudden cat-spring flips the branch away to strike a tree—but the thorn stays in the pad. . .

I had spent more than an hour by the pool and when that story was at last together it was getting dark. It was too late now to go on, but as I turned back I was not regretting the time spent examining the pug marks. They had solved the mystery, and unless I was very wrong the threat to human life had now all but gone, too.

Why? A swarm of flies had said so. All the time I had been examining the swollen pugs the flies had been buzzing over them and crawling round the depressions left by the injured pad. They were finding something more than mud; for Doctor Nature was hard at work and I gave her but a few hours more before she burst the pad and let the thorn come away.

As I walked slowly towards home, I was feeling happier. This new deduction that fitted all the facts so neatly into place was one that particularly pleased me. What was more, the main danger was past; for even if this tiger still hung about he would surely stick to killing cattle and there was not the same desperate urgency to shoot him.

Sometimes even now a shudder runs through me when I think of those thoughts and that muddle-headed complacency. For that deduction was hopelessly wrong, and as I walked home that evening, the Kharnta Tiger was just as dangerous as ever. The one real clue that would have solved the whole riddle was not to be found until a few days later. Then—when it was actually in my hands—I tossed it carelessly away because I failed to find any meaning in it whatsoever. . .

■

Early the next morning I took some of the baits across the river and tied them about the jungles on the other side. If the tiger killed one, I should use the chance to get him out of the way for he was still a menace to our cattle. But for the next three days all the baits stayed alive and there was no news of a kill from anywhere outside. So those signs in the mud had been right: the thorn in the tiger's pad had come away and he was gone to resume his normal life. On the third evening, I brought the baits back from across the river.

The next morning my complacency was rudely shattered. The shouting, when I first heard it, was far away in the distance.

The time then was just after dawn and I was sipping an early cup of tea. It was too soon for any of our labour to be on their way to work and skylarking as they came; but the shouting was coming rapidly nearer, and when it was almost up to the house the sound of feet racing up the drive joined it. I put down my cup and went out to see what was going on. Outside the veranda, I found two excited men breathless from running. They were cartmen, and when they were able to speak they told me that the tiger was still with us. Where he had been and what he had done for the past three days no one will ever know. But from the cartmen's story it was pretty certain that he had not eaten; and now, driven to desperate measures, he had discovered the possibilities of the lonely forest track that leads from the main road out to the tiny village of Anjandana and beyond.

Some of the story of that first bold attack came from the cartmen and the rest I pieced together later. For most of the previous day and night, the tiger had lain hidden behind some rocks close to the track. Starving and in great pain, there was no doubt of what he intended to do. This track is a lonely one and carries only a few men on foot and an occasional bullock-cart bound for market. Whether any men on foot passed by the tiger that day will never be known. Perhaps a kindly fate kept them away for the tiger remained hidden behind the rocks until somewhere around midnight. By now he must have been at the end of his tether and ready for anything: somehow he had to eat soon or die.

Then he heard them. At first it was just a low rumble in the distance: six carts heavily laden with timber. They were still a mile down the track with two hours to go to reach the main road. The only light on the convoy flickered from a smoke-dimmed lantern swaying from the shafts between the leading bullocks. The only driver awake was in the first cart, the other five were huddled under blankets fast asleep.

Suddenly the leading cart jerks to a stop.

A tiger is standing across the track. In the feeble rays of the lantern, his eyes reflect a dull fire. For a few seconds nothing moves. Then the little world in the flickering circle of light explodes.

With a bellowing roar the tiger feints at the left bullock. Both the yoked animals rear madly back and then plunge away to the side of the track with the cart swaying wildly after them. Within a few yards, the cart smashes into a tree and slams to a stop. The bullocks, snorting with terror, strain like maniacs to break the thin rope harnessing them to the yoke. A moment later one wrenches free and goes crashing away into the black jungle screaming with fear.

The tiger has it a second after. But the kill is clumsy: the wretched bullock's dying groans haunt the night for nearly a minute. . .

Not long after I had heard the drivers' story I was hurrying along the track, a part of which keeps to a low ridge of hills running across the north corner of the estate. After a short search, I found the remains of the bullock. Then I found the rocks where the tiger had hidden. Behind him he had left two clues, and it was one of these that immediately changed my mind for the second time about this tiger's injury. The second clue was the key to the whole mystery.

The two things lay close together on a patch of well-trampled grass behind the rocks. The first was a ball of light-coloured hair, still sticky and wet. The tiger had been licking at his injury, but as I was examining the ball of hair a sudden thought struck me, *How could hair come from the bottom of his pad?* Obviously it could not have come from there—which meant that there was another injury either about his body or his legs. That put me back to the theory I had started with, a bullet wound in the shoulder; the thorn, which was certainly in his foot or had been, was pure coincidence and had only made matters worse.

The other thing was a small piece of wood about four inches long. It was well chewed and bloody, and when I picked it up I went back to the dead bullock. The heads of these animals are often decorated with feathers, beads, and other kinds of ornaments. The slip of wood I was holding had once been round and about the size of a thick pencil. It seemed to me that it must have formed part of an ornament which had got mixed up with the tiger's meal. There was, however, nothing else like it about the bullock's head or neck; perhaps whatever it was had been torn off either during the flight from the cart or when the tiger was killing. Anyway, it was obviously of no importance and when I had had another look at it I tossed it down beside the carcass.

When I returned to the track I set off to find signs of the direction in which the tiger had gone. The story I had heard about the previous night's attack was one that held out a great deal of hope. A hope indeed that was almost a promise which said that to this track the tiger would return and that somewhere along it he could be found and shot.

■

It is seven o'clock in the evening two days later. Over to the west the dying sun is just showing above the purple line of the hills. I am moving slowly through a darkening jungle towards the track which is now about a mile ahead. Walking beside me is Bhutu, the same one who came with me to shoot the Laughing Leopard. In front of us lumber two hefty bulls—Ajax and Mars. These two are trained stalkers and are often used about the fields at night to get us up to marauding animals after our crops. Now they are harnessed to a double yoke and there is a lantern swinging underneath it.

We should have started this game before. But I had believed that the tiger, because of his wounds, would not show up again until he was hungry. That assumption had been wrong. He took another bullock last night, one from a string of carts going home from market—the drivers still unaware of the first attack and thus completely unprepared for what was waiting for them down the track.

Now, however, until this tiger is dead, no more carts will be using the track. The tiger's trick of panicking bullocks to force them from the yokes is known to all. So Bhutu and I are off to play 'carts' and we are hoping that the tiger will turn up and try to panic our bulls. But Ajax and Mars won't panic for they are very different from the docile bullocks which draw the carts. These two are full of fight and will stand fast, for the smell of tiger in the dark is nothing new to them.

They have been broken the hard way. Around the fields at home we use them with an implement like an old wooden plough with a difference: the pointed shear stays clear of the ground until the handle is pressed down. If there is trouble about, the point is dropped and digs into the earth: an anchor that even Ajax and Mars find hard to break away from.

Tonight, though, we do not have this implement with us.

On the hard surface of the track it just would not work; but this is something we have not told Ajax and Mars because their toughest job yet might lie just ahead. But if only they knew it, all that is between them and Bhutu is a thin rope tied to their nose-strings. . .

The hands of my watch are pointing to ten-thirty. Ever since we reached the track we have been moving slowly along it while the light from the lantern swinging under the yoke has kept the long black shadows of our legs tramping beside us. We do not like either the darkness or the wind. Visibility is only the few yards to the limit of the flickering light; the wind dulls our hearing and is conjuring up a tiger behind every waving shadow.

But there has been no real sign of the tiger yet, for since we started the jungle on each side of the track has been peaceful and quiet. Even so, that does not mean he is not around: he may still be lying up or moving with a great deal of caution; it is also possible that we have not yet attracted his attention.

Midnight. We are now four miles farther down the track towards Anjandana. Just before we reach a crossing over a dry nullah, I signal Bhutu to stop and he reins in the bulls with a low clucking. We stand listening for ten minutes. There is still nothing that tells us of a tiger on the move; all we hear is the wind sighing through the trees and the howl of jackals in the distance. Is it worth going farther along the track?

We decide no: a few hundred yards on will bring us into open country which extends for more than three miles and we do not think it likely that the tiger will be there. Bhutu prods the bulls round and we start back; as we move off the shadows of our legs fall into step beside us.

As we plod on behind the swaying rumps of the bulls, I am conscious of a vague nagging in my mind. It has been there almost since we started and I feel that something is wrong.

For several minutes I try to find out what is worrying me as I stare down at the bulls' hooves clopping softly into the fine dust on the track. All at once I know what it is. I fall back some forty yards until I can just hear the clopping hooves. *Of course!* With my own rubbers and Bhutu's bare feet dead silent we are not making enough noise—and the tiger will be listening for carts. And if his wounds are giving him the hell I think likely, he will not be doing much moving about: he will be lying tight until he *hears* his victim coming. To do that he does not need to be near the track; with ears as sharp as his he may well be a considerable way off it—far enough to be missing the flickering rays of our lantern as well.

As this is going through my mind I realize that we have forgotten something else. Ajax and Mars, when they are hunting at home, never carry bells. Now they ought to have them; to attract the tiger we should be tinkling along the track like a cart bound for market. I stop Bhutu and whisper what I am thinking. He nods his head slowly. Then, before answering, he pokes the bulls on with the butt-end of his axe. We have been moving for a couple of minutes before a laconic whisper says, '*Why didn't you think of that earlier?*'

I don't answer him, but I do begin to wonder why he is driving the bulls faster. There is no point in asking; he's a phlegmatic type and if he has any reason he will tell me only when he is good and ready.

Suddenly the bulls stop dead and I see Bhutu pointing over to the left.

The abrupt stop catches me unawares and my heart gives a double bound. Then my eyes are straining out of my head and leaping from one prancing shadow to another as the swinging lantern dances them about. But I can see nothing. There is no sign of a tiger and for a fleeting second my eyes flick back to Bhutu. He is still pointing, but in the dim light I get the odd impression that he is a little bored and quite unconcerned.

'*Where is he?*' I hiss.

'Over there—'

Now I see it. A dim shape just catching the outer rays of our lantern. A loaded bullock-cart abandoned by the track.

'*Idiot!* I thought you had seen the tiger.'

'No, sahib. We want a cart and there it is.'

It lies just off the track, its wooden axle torn from the mooring pins, the left wheel jammed against the body. It is the first cart wrecked by the tiger, and as we set about unloading it Bhutu tells me that the driver owned only two bullocks and had been forced to leave the cart here after one was killed because nobody would lend him another to take it away.

The repairs take only ten minutes. All we need are four wooden pegs which Bhutu quickly fashions with his axe. When these are in place and the axle straight, Ajax and Mars are put in the yoke and the cart is back on the track with Bhutu driving while I walk behind. Our progress now is noisy indeed. The empty cart is bouncing in and out of deep ruts with loud bangs and much rattling from its wooden rails; the iron tyres are slapping into stones and grinding noisily through the occasional patches of gravel. We are 'tinkling', too; a string of bells was found hanging on the shafts—the property of the tiger's first victim.

■

It is now a few minutes after four in the morning. It seems much later for the night has been a long one and we are now very tired and covered with a fine film of dust. Not once have we seen or heard any sign of the tiger and the excitement of the first few hours has passed. Monotony is starting to dull our senses and for the past half-hour my mind has begun to wander away from the job on hand. Idle thoughts are jumping in quick succession from one thing to another. Odd problems about the farm . . . what *really* set this tiger off . . . and for what does the inscrutable Bhutu actually want the advance of pay he asked me for when we were mending the cart? Is it to buy that old muzzle-loading gun as he says, or is it for an almighty bender on illicit hooch?

I am wondering, too, about the number of nights we shall have to keep this game up. I decide that we are probably wasting our time no matter how often we do it. The tigers you *have* to shoot are seldom easy ones, and it is surprising how often they seem to offer a certain chance by some unorthodox method. You always try the old way because you think it is going to work, but if you shoot the tiger at all, it is usually on some occasion when you least expect to.

What we need now is a cup of tea to wake us up. After that we can start for home. When I signal to Bhutu he stops the bulls and then unslings the flask he has been carrying over his shoulder. We sit on the verge by the side of the track in silence and sip the strong tea. Ajax and Mars have found some grass along the edge and are cropping it. After refilling the cups I find my cigarettes and offer one to Bhutu; he shakes his head and lights one of his pungent bidis. We sit on for another fifteen minutes in silence.

All at once the night seems very dark. When I look about I see that the bulls are forty yards down the track and our lantern has gone with them. We had better move on. After screwing the cap on the flask I hand it to Bhutu and we start to our feet.

The next few seconds are very confused. The tiger's roar seems to burst in our ears. Hard on it comes a heavy thud and a bellow from Ajax. A moment later there is a loud splintering of wood and the lantern is smashed out.

As I flick the safety-catch off the rifle an appalling din is shattering the night. The bulls seem to be flinging the cart all over the track and bellowing at the top of their lungs. I race forward a few yards and then snap on the torch. The beam shoots out and shows a blur of movement in the middle of a cloud of dust. The sudden light stops the flurry like a sharp word of command. Ajax is on the ground with the tiger on top of him. The next second the light whips the tiger round and he stands staring into the beam.

I get a vivid impression of blazing eyes in a striped mask and a glaring white chest. The foresight is a brilliant dot in the light and centred on the patch of white between the tiger's shoulders. A squeeze on the trigger and a blinding flame explodes from the muzzle of the rifle.

Without a sound the tiger springs high in the air. For a moment, he is out of the narrow circle of light. A slight swing and the beam finds him again as he slams to the ground and sprawls on the verge just off the track.

Ajax, still bellowing, hurtles to his feet and then with his horns down starts pawing angrily at the ground. Mars, with the wreckage of the yoke festooned about his neck, rushes up and stands beside him. But the tiger is dead. The shot has raked him from his chest to the root of his tail.

Once we have made sure that there is actually no life left in him, we have a look at Ajax. Blood is streaming down his rear legs and over his rump, and across his back are long raking claw marks. What seems to have saved his life was the yoke: when the tiger's fangs flashed for his neck one of them dented the top beam while the other gashed into his flesh.

When Ajax is as comfortable as we can make him we turn back to the tiger. We look first for an old bullet wound, but although our search is thorough we find no sign of one; the only hole in the skin is the one just made by the .375 in the chest.

'The kharnta in his foot must be the only wound after all,' remarks Bhutu. Ever since I found that there was a thorn in this tiger's pad everyone has been calling him the Kharnta Tiger. Bhutu lifts the heavy paw while I shine the light on it. It is still swollen to a monstrous size and feels very hot; the whole leg is swollen too and about six inches above the paw there is a patch of bare flesh with an angry red tear in it. I run a finger over the pad and it snags against something sharp. I tell Bhutu to open his knife and to be ready to take out no ordinary thorn.

Ten minutes later Bhutu has it out and I see that the old man from the village was right after all. But he was wrong about his rogues, for even though none of them owns a gun, at least one of them did try for a tiger skin. The wicked little thing in my hand is a crude arrow-head. . .

In case I have left the clue of the chewed piece of wood too obscure, let me clear it up by saying that it was a part of the arrow-shaft. On the night the tiger was wounded, the arrow had been shot almost straight downwards from a tree. It missed the tiger's body but had sliced into his leg just above the paw and the head had penetrated to his pad. The tiger would have bitten the shaft off within seconds of the arrow striking him, but he had not been able to worry out the first four inches left in his leg until the night he lay behind the rocks near the track.

The noise like a stick striking the trunk of a tree? About that I am not so sure, but for what it is worth my theory is that it was made by the bowstring. Many of the bows used in our jungles have double strings with a small strip of wood, two inches or so long, to keep them apart at the centre and to which the arrow is notched. With the strings drawn right back for full power with an extra long arrow this strip of wood almost certainly would fly forward and strike the bow. That is the only answer I can think of that seems to fit. However, it should not be forgotten that the whole village might have been in the plot, and when it misfired a hurried council might have decided that with a touch of mystery the crime might seem to lie on the shoulders of the forest devils—always well able to look after themselves. Choose which solution you like.

JOE

This affair was rummy. That is the only word I can find that really describes it and you will probably agree it's the right one when you know what happened. It took place one night during the rains when I was after a large wild boar. I should have killed him, too, because he gave me an easy shot at forty yards. But he got clean away, saved by an audacity and cunning that were right outside my experience.

Just how I had managed to lose him I did not at once understand, but when that boar got away I was left with a load of trouble which was to last many months. For this brute was a killer which had already ripped and trampled one man to death, and because he was the worst type of bad-tempered 'singler' he would kill again whenever he was caught in the wrong mood.

When this boar first appeared, the rains were well advanced and our crops at the stage when they had started to draw wild pigs and deer in numbers. The nightwatchmen, which normally we use to keep marauding animals away, had started work ten days before. These are stolid chaps who sit on raised platforms in the fields and try to keep them clear with an astonishing medley of noises. Usually they are quite efficient, and it takes something out of the ordinary to disturb them—something, for instance, like the sudden arrival of a man-eating tiger.

It was certainly unfortunate that a tiger's arrival had coincided with the boar's and for some time there was no little confusion. But the real culprit was the boar. He killed the man we found across the river as the deep tracks about the mangled body testified. Even so, although I was sure of that myself, I convinced nobody else, with the result that all the nightwatchmen left their fields. That was awkward. The crops now were wide open to every marauder from the forests. To leave them for even a few nights might well see them completely wiped out. There was no alternative but to guard the fields myself and so I started to go round them at night with a rifle.

I cannot pretend that I liked these night patrols at all. Indeed, I dislike them so heartily that I looked round at once for some way to make them more bearable. There were about 100 acres that were really vulnerable, for not only were these down to peanuts, but they were in fields scattered haphazardly about the forests. I soon decided that what I needed most was lights; then people to take the edge off loneliness and fear when going round in the dark.

The lights were easy, and dozens of hurricane lanterns spread about the crops gave me a lot more confidence. The people were a little more difficult: the only sort I could have were scarecrows, but because I wanted them as much for company as to discourage the pigs, they would have to be realistic. I turned down the crossed-sticks and turnip-headed variety altogether. Mine must be the Madame Tussaud's kind: scarecrows that would make a pig pause and apologize and then push off with a polite tip of his hat. With this sort I could pass the time of night, discuss the crops, slang the government, cuss the weather and exchange the local gossip.

We had a lot of fun making them.

Cupboards, forgotten trunks and bottom drawers were ransacked for old clothes until fourteen colourful figures leaned against the garage wall. Even though we said it ourselves, they were good. A little mixed, perhaps, for there were civilian types jostling military, and one female of such a coarse and blowsy appearance that she would inevitably be an awful warning to the sows.

By the time the last one was finished, they each had a name. But right from the start, my favourite was Joe. He was a military man smartly dressed in an old red mess-jacket and a bush hat. His nose was a well-nourished scarlet, and just below it there sprouted a fiercely waxed handlebar moustache. As his medals showed he was a veteran of many wars, and although his present haircut would have drawn a sharp whistle and a curt 'on a charge' from his old sergeant-major, he was obviously a real old soldier of the Queen, '. . . red coat, smasher "at an" all.'

There were two other reasons why I particularly liked Joe. Firstly, he was by far the most vigilant and resourceful of them all: his fields were generally clear of pigs and I often wondered why. Then, one night as I was going round the fields, I discovered his secret. Joe was *alive!* From a little distance off it was quite uncanny. The movements were distinct, but slow and rather stiff like those of a tired sentry towards the end of his spell of duty. Fascinated, I watched for some minutes hardly daring to move closer in case a gruff, *'Alt! Who goes there?* sent me flying back to the house. A few moments later, I saw them in the light of Joe's lantern. Rats. They were running along his arm and jumping to the ground; others were running up and disappearing into a hole just above his collar. A little investigation showed that Joe's head was full of peanuts filched from the fields.

But I did not disturb the cache. To have a real live scarecrow was something I had not even dreamed of, and after that night I spent more time round Joe than any of the others. That undoubtedly was why I became so fond of him even though I more than suspected that he often played the 'old soldier' on parade. There were several occasions when I thought I smelt strong shag tobacco as I crept up to him out of the dark; and on one visit I was ready to swear he was humming 'Dolly Grey' until he saw me coming.

There was also another reason why I particularly like Joe, and that was because he saved my life.

However, before that happened I had been on the night rounds for some time. I had also killed a lot of pigs, but I was losing far more than I shot at for the most annoying of reasons. Time and again I was being let down at critical moments by the torch mounted on the rifle. The trouble was the batteries. They would fizzle out with no warning, and as they were coming from our local weekly bazaar—where almost anything can happen—I came to the conclusion that I was buying either old or second-hand stock. Indeed, right from the start the behaviour of the ones I had been getting was always problematical: they might last two nights or just two minutes. The last lot of six had been consistently bad.

In the end I decided to go to the bazaar on the next Wednesday to see for myself. Up till then I had been sending a servant, but it had occurred to me that if this chap had a torch (and a fiddle) of his own, the trouble might well lie here. Now

I should be able to check on him, or perhaps discover if there was any trickery going on in the bazaar.

These weekly bazaars are colourful occasions which few of the local inhabitants like to miss. For here, after the work a day week, is life: thronging, jostling people; noise, enticing smells, and a golden chance to exchange gossip. Dozens of little stalls are laid out along the dusty main street and at them the simple villagers can buy almost everything they know about. Rich and gaudy sweetmeats, fancy footwear decorated with gold and silver thread, glass bangles in all colours of the rainbow, cheap dyed handkerchiefs, bright shirts, scarves of every hue; and trinkets from a dull metal mirror to an imitation wrist-watch. Through it all weave the gay saris of the women and the bright turbans of the men, moving in an atmosphere warm and heavy with the rich scent of spices and exotic fruits.

The law is here, too. Every Wednesday we get one policeman, not so much to deter likely crimes of pilfering as to watch for the demon drink since these are Prohibition days and our district is quite dry [sic]. This week our policeman is rather an untidy one in a grubby tunic and a forage cap worn with such a swagger that it perches across the top of his head from ear to ear and imparts a vaguely Napoleonic air. As none of his superiors is within several miles, he has removed his boots so that his puttees end with a huge pair of splay-toed feet which give the effect of a deliberately meant comic touch to his outfit. Even so, there is something of sinister arrogance in the bearing of this seeming buffoon. He is a big man sporting a heavy black moustache with a fierce curl; his face is a dark scowl as with thumbs crooked in belt he watches the milling crowd.

He's looking for 'likker'. And he knows it is here; for these days most of the forest folk have become moonshiners and brew up fiery spirits from a variety of jungle fruits and flowers to supply an ever-growing demand. This bazaar is one of the main links to the consumer.

I watch the policeman as he goes to work. He first peers suspiciously into some of the stalls, shakes a brass vessel here and taps an earthen one there. All at once he swings round to some passers-by who have stopped to gape and, without even a 'pardon me', he prods them about the body with a dirty finger. He has hardly finished this when he suddenly spins round and pounces on a little chap with a bicycle and lets the air out of both tyres. He scores a miss, but offers no apology beyond unclipping the pump and handing it to his victim. There is no comment from the crowd: everybody knows that he might have been right because hooch is often brought in and out in cycle tubes.

All this time the *real* business—as this hero knows very well—is going on in the back streets of the bazaar. But you won't find him going round there. Why should he? Our policeman today is a 'square one' and the bootleggers have cut him in to keep his nose in the main street where he can do both sides a bit of good by looking out for the bilkers that have not kicked in with their protection money. If he does that, and otherwise plays fair, there are other sweeteners to come before he goes home: not a few powerful snifters under that badly polished belt. The pantomime comes when these are going down as the bazaar closes; for both he and the bootleggers must keep his self-importance well inflated, and it is tacitly understood that these snifters are part of his business. From the first sample tot to the last there will be much sucking at that fierce moustache, and a loud smacking of lips as his eyes roll upwards in exaggerated concentration. He's testing for full flavour. The public can rest content; he is here to protect them by making quite sure that no one is being *really* naughty by watering the stuff down.

But I have not come to the bazaar to buy liquor. I am here after batteries and I want good ones. A little way down the lane of stalls is a man squatting on the ground with two trays of them; one is in front and the other by his side, half hidden behind his back. As I buy razor blades from a stall, I watch him covertly and see two customers served from the tray by his side. He greeted the customers like old friends and when one reached for the front tray he was waved quickly away and a low conversation followed which ended in a raucous guffaw from the customer. Here is the answer to my bad batteries: suckers to the front, wise guys round the side.

I approach him with the confident step of a wise guy, reach down and take four batteries from the side tray. He looks up quickly with a shadow of annoyance on his face. But when he sees me he smiles: 'Not those, sahib. They are no good at all. Take from here.' He holds out four from the other tray.

I shake my head, hand him the right price, and walk away. He gets up and comes running after me: 'No, no, sahib!' he protests, trotting along by my side. '*Those* batteries will give you no light at all!' Then lowering his voice, '*They* were bought only for the lead if they could not be sold as they are—a matter of business, you understand. But you, sahib, are different. I will give *you* only the best, so be so good as to exchange those for these and enjoy *good* illumination!'

He has by now confirmed all my suspicions and I tell him to go away. But he refuses to take no for an answer and trails along close behind begging me to change the batteries and 'ensure such light as only the sun can give'. At last I get annoyed and threaten to call the policeman to take him away. Just for a moment he seems a little scared. Then he pulls one of the oldest tricks in the game. But it's a trick that now leaves me quite unmoved because I can no longer be shamed into giving way. With a quick movement he snatches the turban from his head and dashes it angrily to the ground. At the same time he calls loudly to the crowd around to witness how a poor man has been cheated by the rich sahib '. . . taking my best batteries and paying me nothing like their proper worth. He has "hit me in the stomach" and so I shall surely starve to death!'

I ignore him, walk to the end of the bazaar for some cigarettes, then saunter slowly back. He is now packing up his wares and as I pass he shoots me one of the dirtiest looks I have ever received. 'You have driven a poor man away from the bazaar!' he shouts after me. A slight overstatement, I thought. But it's all part of the game and as soon as I'm out of sight he'll start to unpack. . .

■

When I left the house that evening to go round the fields it was raining. Up above the low-lying clouds, a full moon was filtering dimly through them and taking some of the blackness out of the night. The alarms started almost at once, telling of either a tiger or a leopard on the prowl. First with the news was a spotted deer somewhere down near Monkey's Folly.

WOW-ou! WOW-ou!

Twice the high-pitched call came clearly above the whispering rain, carrying a chilling note. As the calls died away, an ominous silence settled on the jungle broken only by the rustle of leaves and the plaintive cries of plovers wheeling above the river. Walking slowly round I could feel an electric tension in the air: every animal in the forest was on the alert with senses searching desperately for the danger. All at once a sambur hind gave us another clue with her sharp grating rasp of alarm. The terror had moved towards Creaking Tree Hill.

Most of that night the pigs were very watchful. Indeed, there were not so many about as usual and those I heard did not show themselves for a shot. Towards four-thirty in the morning, the alarms died down. Whatever it was that had been on the prowl had either passed on or was now busy on a kill. A little later the weather started to clear; before a freshening breeze the clouds broke up to unveil the star-studded sky as they scudded away.

By the time I had completed my fourth round and was back in the Long Field, the night seemed so peaceful and quiet that I decided to have a rest and a smoke. I sat down on an old stump and filled my pipe. Away down the field I could see Joe, a bright splash of scarlet in the winking light of his lantern. He nodded a welcome and I waved back idly wondering as I did what his old sergeant would have thought about such behaviour on parade: 'acting in a manner unsoldierly' was what he would probably have put on the charge sheet. . .

All at once I heard it. At first, it was just a faint crashing through the forest from across the far side of the field. But it was coming nearer fast, the confident approach of some large animal. I sat up and stared over. A few moments later, a teak sapling was shaken violently against the skyline as a heavy body barged past it. Then I heard the crack of twigs and a great rustling as an animal broke through the brush fringing the forest. It was still masked by the black shadows from the trees but now it was swishing through the tall grass verge. At last I picked up movement and the next second a vast black bulk was coming towards the field.

A huge boar. He put his head down at once and began to root up the peanuts with noisy, contented grunts. He was about sixty yards off—a little too far for a certain kill with a torchlight shot. An old and experienced boar will seldom if ever stand for a light; he knows that there is a man with a gun behind it and he will jink out of the beam the second it is switched on. But if he's a killer he doesn't always run away: moments later he may tear in from a flank like a galloping horse. This boar has not done that yet, although he has had two chances: we have met twice before and on each occasion I have shot at him—a clean miss both times.

The boar was moving nearer to the light thrown by Joe's lantern. It looked as though he had been round Joe before and knew exactly what he was. For a few moments I saw him a little clearer as a patch of lighter clouds passed across the moon: a powerful brute with a great hump of bristles on his neck. As he moved closer to Joe's lantern, I got an occasional wink from his tushes as he crunched at the nuts. I want to be sure of him, and the only way I can be sure is to get closer.

I got up from the stump and crept away to make a detour round the field. From the other side I could get to within thirty yards of him. The boar was making so much noise with the nuts that it was easy to move quite fast and still not attract his attention. I was almost up to where I wanted to get when I remembered the torch. The batteries had been well-used all night and were now running down. But the new ones I had bought in the bazaar were in my pocket and so I stopped to change them over. With this boar there must be no hitch to give him a chance for reprisals; for the few seconds he would allow me I wanted to put on him all the light I could get.

With the batteries changed, I crept forward a few yards and then stopped. The boar had moved away from the light of Joe's lantern and was about forty yards off. But I could still see him, a large black mound against the lighter leaves of the peanuts. I raised the rifle and got on him as best I could in the dark and took the first pressure off the trigger; then I slowly slid the switch of the torch forward.

Nothing happened. Not even a glimmer. With the rifle still to my shoulder I screwed up the base of the torch tighter. The switch slid forward again but there was still no result. I lowered the rifle quickly and started to press and squeeze round the case of the torch; a loose contact had given trouble before and this had cured it. By now I was sweating blood in case the wind changed and the boar scented me.

Suddenly I knew that there was something seriously wrong. Something wet and cold was dripping out of the torch and soaking my left hand. What it was I could not imagine, but it could be coming from nowhere except the batteries. I was too close to put back the old ones; a boar's hearing is acute and I did not want to toss away the advantage of surprise—and be caught without a light.

It was too dark to see the sights on the rifle. But I could not afford to let this boar go free, and it seemed to me that he was close enough to take a chance. By extending my left hand right along the barrel and holding up a finger I had a rough foresight. Taking plenty of time I put this on the dark blur of the boar and slowly squeezed the trigger. As the rifle crashed he leaped in the air with a startled screech. For a moment I lost him after the jolt of recoil. Then I saw a black mound haring across the peanuts and making straight for Joe.

No wonder. Joe was the only *living* thing in sight. I watched with a queer thrill fluttering round my stomach for the old soldier was nodding and waving his lamp to draw the enemy to himself.

The maddened beast rushed into the feeble circle of light. I saw his great black body give the characteristic little jump of the attacking boar. The shock of the charge slammed Joe to the ground and his lantern snuffed out to the tinkle of shattering glass. Through the darkness I heard the murder as vicious tushes slashed at the body and furious hooves trampled it into the earth.

I was still listening when the boar's temper cooled. He had probably decided that he was wasting his time, but he was still savage when he moved away towards the other side of the field. I let him go: after what I had just heard I hadn't the courage to take him on again without a light.

As I walked home for another torch I was feeling rather shaken. I was also puzzled and more than a little annoyed because I had wounded a dangerous animal which would now have to be followed up. That might prove to be more fun than I wanted; that badly placed bullet would not have improved his temper and he was certain to give all the trouble he could before he died. I was also wondering what was wrong with the batteries I had bought in the bazaar.

When I got them back to a light, I soon found out. For a few moments, though, I could hardly believe my eyes. But my nose confirmed what I was seeing and also told me that I had after all cheated the chap in the bazaar. These batteries *were* worth more than his others because each one held a sizeable slug of 'Old Horsey'.

Old Horsey. . . ?

Well, that's what we call it, but the locals have a rude and much more expressive term for what is actually cheap and nasty Indian rum.

It was cleverly done. Two of the cells I had were the ordinary lead ones cleaned out; the other two had been made up out of tin. They had then been filled with rum and cunningly resealed with pitch on top of a cardboard disc. This was strengthened with the original electrode steadied on a few blobs of lead to make up weight. Slipped back into the maker's cardboard jackets they would pass all but a close scrutiny. Each battery held a useful tot of rum: just a nice convenient nip for an exhausted shopper.

A rummy business indeed. And I have no doubt that our untidy policeman would have reported to his superior (also interested in the rake-off) that there was no liquor in the bazaar that Wednesday that *he* didn't know about. . .

NEVER BE TOO SURE . . .

He was a badmash leopard. In other words, a sneaking rogue who had spent his life haunting the forest villages like a fleeting yellow ghost. As silent as the waving shadows, he was always about at the wrong time to pick off unwary stragglers from flocks of goats and herds of cattle. With the passing years he had developed an amazing cunning which was now combined with an incredible boldness through long familiarity with man.

When he came to us he was not really unexpected. Leopards, as a general rule, like to settle down in one spot and make that area their own. There, once they are in, they strongly resent any intrusion from their own kind. Strangely enough, though, for there are few more wicked beasts than these, they usually respect another bad man's territory and seldom poach until the rightful owner has either moved away or been destroyed. That was how we got the badmash. We had a 'vacancy' for I had just shot a leopard which had been playing hell for some time.

Within a week of his arrival the badmash was really in business. He began by clawing his way into a chicken run where he killed sixty-three chickens. The next night he was back and in again, despite a ring of lanterns round the runs. Then he killed two young bulls. He got the first by waiting *inside* an outlying cattle shed for the herd to come home; he got the second by waiting outside, hidden round the corner, for the same herd to go out.

The following night, I tied a goat in the jungle at a spot near water he was likely to visit. He was pretty certain to take this tempting supper, and if all went well I meant to make it his last meal. But although he passed close to the bait several times he left it alone, a clear indication that he preferred his food 'without any strings'.

That was disappointing. But soon after ten o'clock the next morning, one of the men in charge of the cattle came racing up to the house with the news that a leopard was circling the herd. I ran down with a rifle and began stalking through the jungle that fringes the grasslands where the cattle were grazing. They were all very restless, the cows keeping their calves close beside them. An hour later, when I was almost ready to give it up, the leopard sneaked out from some cover sixty yards off.

He saw me at once and jerked into a swift crouching run with the white flash of his belly scraping the grass as he streaked for a patch of brush. It was an awkward shot, but I saw him jump to it and swing up his tail. A hit, but I was fairly sure it had been far back and by the way he went, probably no more than a glancing clip.

All that day I tried to find him again. But there was not a trace of blood nor any other sign to put me on his trail. When it got too dark to see I reluctantly gave it up, worried to have an animal about the estate that might be badly hurt and which could now be dangerous.

When I got back to the house, I was met with the news that a young bull had not returned home. Next morning, it was found dead lying under a tree in the jungle. A part had been eaten from the neck and a little off the hindquarters. In spite of my bullet, the badmash seemed as active as ever.

The loss of that bull brought one consolation: the leopard would surely return for another feed and I meant to be there when he arrived. That day Bhutu had not turned up for work, so I sent Mitu, another good shikari, to put up a machan and tie the kill down.

Almost always I go myself to look things over, but that morning I had some outside work which would keep me away until a problematical 'some time after lunch'. Mitu, however, is a good man and I felt sure that he would have everything ready for a sit-up early that evening. But all that day I was badly delayed and eventually got home late. In fact, it was almost dusk before I set off with Mitu for the kill, carrying a rifle and a spare torch slung around my neck. By the time we reached the dead bull, it was nearly dark. There was no time to check arrangements properly and I had to be satisfied with a quick look all round.

As Mitu walked away, I took rapid stock of my position from the machan before the last of the light faded. I was in a large tree with deep shadows beneath its spread. The kill was lying in a clear space in front and below me about twenty feet away. Behind me, and coming right up to the trunk of the tree, was a thick clump of lantana bushes. The machan was simply a small wooden seat tied to the lower branches some ten feet above the ground. Not as high as I should have liked when dealing with a wounded leopard which would surely creep up without any noise and be full of suspicion. Beyond the kill was a well-worn game-path leading to a deep nullah which held a pool of water, a drinking spot for scores of jungle animals.

Soon it was dark. In the distance I could still hear Mitu singing lustily as he went home, not only to mislead the leopard but to warn off 'mischievous forest devils' if any were about. Settling down into the most comfortable position I could find, I began to wait for the badmash to arrive. I felt sure he would not be long. Leopards nearly always come before nine o'clock, and a bold one like this had probably been hanging around quite close all day. Indeed, so sure was I of a short vigil that I had promised Babs to be back for a late dinner 'somewhere around ten'.

An hour dragged by with no suspicious sound from the jungle. The darkness now was intense; there was no moon and angry black clouds were growling across the sky threatening a storm; the kill was invisible and I could barely see my hand a few inches from my face. Except for the chirping insects, the forest all round was silent. That, however, did not mean a thing: when the leopard came it would be without warning. A sharp shower that morning had soaked the ground and left it like a soft carpet; and the fallen leaves that had been tinder dry before the rain, crackling and rustling underfoot, were now soggy and trod in without a sound.

Five minutes to ten and still no sign of the quarry. I was getting a little cramped and beginning to think of dinner, a thought that left me slightly annoyed because I was not sitting for fun. Indeed, everything we had done up to this moment had been the ordinary routine drill to deal with an expensive pest, and I regard these vigils now—whether they last an hour or all night—as 'just another chore about the farm'.

Another half-hour passed in silence, and I was almost ready to give up when things started to happen. And although I didn't know it then, the next seven hours were to be anything but routine.

■

The leopard came quietly. There was just the slightest rustle as he brushed past the bushes at the back of the tree. Then I heard him start to circle slowly, and once or twice he stopped not far from the kill. Although I could see nothing through the inky blackness, I sensed that he was suspicious. It was likely that he had been watching my tree for some time and a tiny movement or sound might have given me away. When he went on circling without coming up to the kill I became more and more sure that he must suspect, *or even know*, that something was perched on the lowest branch.

Suddenly he dived on the kill and tore off a great lump of flesh. The next second he leaped away and I heard him eating a little distance off. When he had finished, he circled twice more and then came in again with a quick dash. He did the same thing several times, a clear indication that something was worrying him. I wondered whether to try for him the next time he came in. I decided not to: his movements were so quick and erratic I might bungle the shot; it was better to wait and hope that he settled down beside the kill.

The next moment I thought I had lost him. He stopped circling and seemed to be moving off, passing through brush a little distance away. Had he gone for good? After nearly three-quarters of an hour without the slightest whisper of him it looked as if this chance had been lost. But no, without the ghost of a warning he was back with a sudden rush from only a few yards away where he had probably been lying all this time. Hard on his pounce came the twang of a tightening rope—a sharp *snap!* as it parted—then the sound of the kill being dragged to the back of the tree.

It seemed deliberate, a taunting gesture which left the leopard perfectly safe. To get a shot now was impossible; he was directly behind me and under the bushes that ran out from the trunk of the tree. From where I was, low on the branch, I would not have seen him, even in daylight, through that tangled mass.

I now heard the leopard settle down to feed beside the kill. That was maddening, yet he was still obviously nervous and frequently broke off his meal to listen. For a few minutes I just sat there wondering what to do. Then that noisy feast going on behind me produced an idea. Could I use those sounds to mask my movements while I climbed farther up the tree? If I could get up high enough and sufficiently far out to look over the edge of the bushes, it might be possible to get a sight of the leopard at his meal.

Before I started, this had seemed a reasonable plan. But to climb a strange tree, silently, on a pitch black night when burdened with a heavy rifle and a torch swinging from your neck is exasperatingly difficult. On this occasion it was to be made even more difficult by the knowledge that just below and listening for the tiniest sound was an already suspicious animal with the keenest pair of ears in the jungle. Hardly daring to breathe, I started to rise slowly on the machan, hours seeming to pass before I was standing on it. For a few moments, I stopped to listen to the leopard feeding. He had not heard me yet, and so with the greatest care I started to climb.

Inching painfully upwards and pausing whenever the feeding stopped, it took a full hour to get up twenty feet. But at the end of that time the leopard was still there and still feeding. The worst of the climb was over. Now, just above me, I could feel a fork in the branch I was on. If I could reach that, the kill should be right below me with the leopard lying close beside it. I started to move, but the second after I did the sound of tearing flesh stopped abruptly and there came a deep throaty growl.

After that things happened fast. I heard the leopard swish through the undergrowth as he padded away from the kill. It seemed to me that he was not unduly hurried and there was more than a hint of sinister purpose in his movements. This was no scared animal running away, for it growled again and then came the sure warning that trouble was breaking when a loud menacing snarl ripped out of the blackness below. Hard on this came the rush of an animal racing through the brush and an instant later the tree shook as a heavy form slammed against the trunk with the noise of ripping claws fighting wildly for a hold on the bark. A few moments after, to a mad threshing of leaves, I thought I heard the leopard drop back to the ground.

As the noise died away, I had no doubt of what had happened. My last effort on the branch must finally have warned the leopard of the danger above him. Normally, this would have scared any such animal away. But this leopard was wounded, and he had realized at last that there was an enemy up the tree he could take his revenge on.

A slight rustling on the ground caught my ears, warning that he might spring up again at any moment. Sweat started to seep out on my palms, for although I was now well out of reach from any direct leap from below, leopards climb like the cats they are and I was in no position to meet an attack from right behind. I was still wrapped round a slim and swaying branch, a perilous perch that gave little chance to use the rifle. I must get up to the fork at once and turn round.

Before I could move, a faint sound set icy fingers plucking at my spine. I froze to the branch. The noise had come from somewhere on the tree not far below me. I listened with my heart pounding, waiting for it to come again. All at once it did, louder and more distinct—the creaking of the rope securing the machan!

With my left hand I snatched at the spare torch and snapped it on, sending the light down and behind me. The beam burst through the leaves with a blinding glare, for a moment searched about them and then steadied. The leopard was sitting on the machan with his forepaws resting on the branch it was tied to.

When the light first picked him up he was staring *straight down at the ground*, his neck stretched sharply forward, the whole attitude one of intense concentration. As the light found him, he relaxed almost lazily and turned his head to look up at the beam. The next few seconds were very confused. I acted instinctively and without regard to the precarious hold I had on the tree. The torch was in my left hand, the rifle in my right, held by the pistol grip and pressed hard against the branch. Almost before I knew it, the rifle was swinging down and the shot was fired as the muzzle swooped past the leopard's blazing eyes.

As the report crashed out, the leopard sprang away and vanished out of the light into the darkness. I nearly followed him, and a few breathless moments went by while I fought to stay up the tree. Once I was comparatively secure, I switched off the torch and began to listen anxiously for more sounds from below.

After the shot, a deep silence had settled on the jungle. From below the tree there was not a sound, nothing moving and no sign of an animal in distress. Had the leopard been hit? And if he had been, was it a fatal wound or just a painful one that would arouse his temper even more? It was reasonable to suppose that he had been hit somewhere for the range had been under twenty feet. So unless he was dead, there was close at hand an extremely angry twice-wounded leopard who would certainly be bent on evening the score. And he now knew the way up the tree as well as I did!

There was a great temptation to search the ground below with the torch: the leopard might be lying dead not far away. But he could also be very much alive, so until I was better placed to meet an attack, it would be unwise to pinpoint my position. Heedless of the noise I scrambled quickly up to the fork, turned round, and then sat in it with my legs dangling down. This was comfortable, and with the rifle across my knee I waited for the badmash to come up again. But the minutes dragged by and became an hour and there was still nothing moving in the jungle below. Such a long interval suggested that the leopard was indeed either dead or scared away for good.

By now, I was longing for a smoke. But I fought the craving back when I remembered how cunning this beast was.

Perhaps he was just being patient and waiting to catch me off guard.

Five minutes later, I heard it. A sound not part of the jungle night but a peculiar noise like some gurgling cough repeated at short intervals and coming from quite far off. Puzzled, I listened hard for several minutes more. At first I could make nothing of it, but gradually it came to me that what I was hearing was an animal vomiting his heart out.

It had to be the leopard, and from the sound of things he was badly wounded. He was not likely to go far now, and even if he lived until daylight it should not be difficult to find him. The vomiting went on for nearly fifteen minutes and then stopped. When another half-hour had gone by with no sound of him I decided to have that smoke; at the same time I was considering whether to go home until day-break. My pipe had been filled and I was feeling for matches, when a sound from below nearly shot me out of the tree. From the kill beneath had come a loud sniff and then a deep satisfied growl.

Surely not . . . ?

But there was no mistaking a big cat at work. And this time he was really down to it, tearing off great lumps of flesh and punctuating the meal with a loud crunch of bones. That vomiting had deceived me completely: the leopard was not wounded, and he had been sick simply because he had bolted his meal the first time.

However, I was now ready to receive him, in a comfortable seat and free to use both arms. He sounded directly beneath me, and with the rifle steady against my thigh I pressed on the torch. The lantana bushes below burst into a blaze of light. But there was no sign of the leopard and the feasting had stopped. A moment later I saw him, two bright eyes had winked through the bushes. He was right underneath them, but peering down I made out a vague form under the tangled mass of leaves and twigs. Where his shoulders were I could only guess, but I took plenty of time and squeezed off a steady shot.

The recoil shook me off him and in that fraction of a second he vanished. But I could hear him crashing through the undergrowth and heading towards the nullah seventy-five yards away. I listened, hoping to mark the spot if he dropped. But he kept going, and I was just beginning to think I had missed again, when I heard a distinct splash. Right after it came the sounds of a heavy animal floundering in water. He was in the pool in the nullah, and what I was hearing could be nothing else but his death throes. A few seconds later, there rose on the still night air a long-drawn-out yowl. It screamed out eerily like some banshee's chilling lament.

Wailing up from the dark jungle, it sent goose-flesh pricking out over my body. I didn't know quite why, but that yowl struck an odd note and left me wondering and puzzled. But I was now sure that the leopard was dead, and so I settled down to wait the remaining half-hour to the dawn.

I must have dozed for about twenty minutes and then woke with a sudden start when I heard the leopard again. He was certainly not dead, and in some miraculous way had doubled back for he was now coming from behind me, the opposite direction from the pool. As he came, he was moaning piteously and obviously very unsteady on his legs.

He was making again for the pool in the nullah, most probably driven back by thirst. I could not see him as he was some way over to the right, but the light now was good enough to shoot by and I started to climb down the tree. When I was on the ground I gave him another two minutes and then started to follow, keeping well to one side of the path that led to the pool. Some trees and bushes grow along the bank overlooking this, and when I reached them I crept to the edge and looked down.

The leopard was there, crouched by the pool on the far side. He did not see me raise the rifle and the bullet took him at the point of the shoulder. Almost wearily, he raised his head towards the sound of the shot before rolling over on his side. Before going down, I threw a stone which landed in the water near his front paws and he did not move.

Now that he really was dead, I jumped and stamped about the bank to shake off the stiffness after the night in the tree. When my circulation was back I slung the rifle and made for the path, some twenty yards to my left, which ran down to the nullah in a steep muddy incline. I was half-way to the bottom of this when I stopped dead, fighting to keep my balance on the slippery slope and unsling the rifle at the same time. There was a tiger almost at my feet under the right bank!

But it was dead, lying on its side with nearly all its body in the shallow water. The pool around it was settled and clear. It had been here for some time.

There was a bullet hole on its back just behind the head, and between the forelegs an open wound where the 'soft-nose' had come out. Here was my second shot, and I saw then for the first time how blind I had been to the odd things that had happened last night: the broken rope . . . the deep sniff over the kill . . . that despairing yowl. All these had said Tiger—but I could imagine nothing but a badmash leopard.

A little investigation showed that the tiger came to the kill by no accident. It was his own, and he had simply returned for another feed. The leopard had been hungry and was there to steal if he could. My bullet the previous day had crippled a hind leg which had made hunting for him difficult. Other signs showed that throughout the night the tiger only came to the kill. But right from the start, he suspected that he was not alone. After a while he had become sure and had then gone to chase the intruder off. After that he returned, broke the rope, and dragged his meal under the bushes at the back of the tree. While I was climbing up the branch, the tiger had been disturbed again. But not by any noise from above: the leopard was still prowling close by.

The tiger left the kill again and snarled out the threats which had alarmed me so much. They had alarmed the leopard still more, for he was well aware that he was in no condition to meet such a powerful enemy even by running away. So he promptly leaped up the nearest tree—without the slightest suspicion that it was already occupied!

My bullet had caught him low in the chest and had raked along his stomach. Although it was a fatal wound, the poor devil lasted all night. But until the morning he had never moved from where I had heard him being sick. This place I found and it showed clearly that he'd had none of the kill. The shot had scared the tiger away until the early hours of the morning. Hunger then drove him back to his meal and the second bullet that killed him. . .

I often think of what might have happened if the tiger had not been dead when I walked down to the nullah. Or suppose that the leopard had appeared first and been shot according to plan. With my chore apparently finished, I should have climbed down and perhaps met the tiger somewhere near his kill. Since that night, I have always tried not to be too sure of anything with leopards and tigers.

DEATH IN SIXTY-FIVE MINUTES

You may perhaps be wondering about the wounded boar which murdered Joe and whether he was ever shot. Actually he was, but I hesitated for a long time before deciding to put the story here because I always feel ashamed whenever I think of that night. However, it is now many years since it happened and a lot of the sting has worn off the memory. And there's another point, too: by telling the story I may perhaps save someone else from the same sort of experience. . .

That boar gave us a great deal of trouble and turned out to be one of the most dangerous animals I have hunted. After wounding him that night, I was out looking for him again as soon as it was light. There was no sign of him anywhere, and nothing to show how badly he was hurt. In the late afternoon, I gave it up and went home for tea and some sleep; at seven o'clock I had to go back to guard the fields.

Three days later the boar appeared again and nearly killed Khanna, the young son of our head gardener. Khanna then was ten years old and had just started to help with the cattle. At midday, when he had finished his meal, he left the herd and went to the river for a drink. The boar caught him half-way down the path to the river-bed. He was badly ripped about the stomach and legs, and what undoubtedly saved his life was the pluck of the other cowherd who ran up when he heard the screams.

Within fifteen minutes of the attack, Bhutu and I had rounded up the cattle and were driving them through a strip of jungle where the boar was still likely to be. The boar, thoroughly used to grazing cattle, would take no notice of them and sit tight. By going in close behind them, we might get right up to him before he saw us.

The boar did sit tight, and although he must have seen me he let me pass within a few yards. Bhutu, some paces behind me, saw under a thick bush a suspicious mound and then the flick of an ear. He whistled—and as I turned the boar charged him. Bhutu swung his axe but was slammed down before the blade fell. It was not possible to shoot. The boar had Bhutu on the ground and was already whipping round after his first rush.

The boar won again. A few seconds later, he was crashing away to safety leaving behind a cursing Bhutu with a badly gashed leg and me with a shattered 12-bore. My only hurt was a scratched calf, but about all the consolation we had was that the boar must have a hell of a headache.

Two days later, three men from Tendukhera were walking along the path by the river when the boar crashed out from cover and raced straight at them. Two got up trees, but the third was badly mauled and only got away alive because more men were on the path a little way behind. This boar now was really dangerous and liable to attack on sight without provocation. That he had not yet killed another man was only because he had not caught one alone.

I began to neglect the fields to sit during the nights at spots the boar was likely to pass. It was a thankless task. In the dark, one pig looks much like another and with the peanuts now at their juiciest there were scores to choose from. Then one morning I got another shot at him when I was on my way to breakfast, with the sun just peeping above the hills. He was crossing the corner of a field at a fast trot and had not seen me because the sun was in his eyes. It was a long shot and had to be taken quickly for he would have been behind cover in a few seconds.

I found a small piece of skin and some fat spattered over a leaf. The bullet had passed clean through him, though it was not possible to tell where; he might or might not be a dying animal. For the rest of that day, he was hunted hard. With eight men, I followed him up behind the cattle. Occasionally there were spots of blood and we were often close to him; but not once did he turn to fight as I was hoping he would. We all heard him several times but no one actually saw him; the thick cover which comes with the rains had allowed him to escape.

A few days later, I had to go out on business. When I returned in the evening, I heard that the boar had been seen again. What a chance missed! If I had been at home that day this story would have ended then, for the boar had been found lying in the open—fast asleep!

Mitu's wife had been out gathering firewood, and when coming back had seen something black in the grass just in front of her. She had only realized what it was when nearly up to it. Fortunately, she is a sensible girl and had had the presence of mind to put her load down quietly and move away fast. However, even in those few seconds she'd had a good look at the boar and was able to tell me that his right hind leg was stiff with blood. And she had seen something else, 'His right tush,' she said, 'is thin and straight and about as long as this—' She picked up an ivory paper-knife which is nine inches long. At the time I put this down to the ordinary exaggeration, for boars showing nine inches of tush happily do not roam our jungles.

Yet, as events proved later, Mitu's wife was nearly right. The boar's left tush, which she had not seen, was normal; the right one was badly deformed, thin and much longer than I had seen before. It was also loose and we were able to pull it out quite easily; for at the base of it, and no doubt the cause, was a squashed lead pellet about the size of a pea—just one of twenty-nine other assorted shot we eventually dug out of the body.

As soon as I had heard her story, I got ready to sit up. Mitu's wife was quite sure that the boar had not heard her. If that was true—and it probably was because boars sleep exceedingly soundly—then it was very likely that he was still where she had left him.

By now it was seven-thirty and dark. Everything, however, was ready. The spot where the boar had been seen was near a game-path leading to the river; this also led back to one of the biggest fields of peanuts. The boar, of course, did not have to use this path back once he had woken up and been to the river for a drink. But the chances were that he would use it because it was the straightest way to a good feed. I was going to chance it, for already built and covering this path was a 'hide' I had used several times before.

When I got to the hide at about eight o'clock, it was a fine night but with only the light from the stars. This hide was a good one; sited under the lee of an overgrown duranta hedge, it had an old piece of corrugated iron above a waist-high framework of stakes interlaced with long leafy shoots from the hedge. It blended perfectly, and if I kept still the boar would never see me.

Nearly two hours had passed before I noticed the black clouds rolling up from the west. They came fast and soon were growling overhead and wiping the stars from the sky. The night grew darker and the whine of the wind rose to a screaming wail. The storm broke with a vivid violet flash and a shattering clap of thunder. The rain came roaring a moment later.

As the fury mounted, I huddled into my chair. In spite of the weather, the hide would keep me snug and dry. But as I listened to the storm rising, I wondered whether to sit on. If the boar came now I should probably miss him; visibility through the dark night and driving rain was only a few feet, and the screaming wind would whip away any sound he might make.

I decided to stay on even though I didn't like the idea at all. The wind was howling in from behind me and veering wildly from side to side. If the boar passed in front, he was pretty sure to scent me. I groped for the rifle leaning against the hide and laid it across my knee; if he picked me up he would come in fast.

The next hour was uncomfortable. I was on tenterhooks the whole time and my ears seemed ready to burst with the strain of listening. The tension eased a few minutes after eleven, when all at once the wind faded to a sighing whisper and the heavy splash of the rain pattered to a gentle drip and then stopped. All I could hear now was the trees unbowing their heads and shaking the water from their leaves. For a short time, an unnatural silence hung over the jungle; then the normal sounds of the night sprang out of the darkness with startling clarity through the rain-washed air. The chirping of cicadas, jackals howling in the distance; dogs barking in Tendukhera across the river.

The black clouds were now scudding away in the wake of the grumbling storm. As they went, they unveiled a star-studded sky set with a sliver of moon. Then the night was luminous; impenetrable darkness had changed to a soft radiance which showed the blurred outline of trees and the dim line of the game-path winding away to the right and left of the hide.

I began to wonder whether the boar had passed in the storm. I thought not, for with a keen nose like his, he would certainly have found me. I sat back in my chair and began to think about him. He carried the scars of two of my bullets and this was the eighteenth time I had sat up for him at night. It was little consolation to know that he had killed a man before I wounded him, for there was no doubt that my two bullets had helped to make him the savage and revengeful animal he was now. I was still thinking about him when a slight rustling came from somewhere behind me. It was on the other side of the hedge, but the sound froze the blood in my veins and set the clammy fingers of fear tapping down my spine. After a few seconds of silence, there came again a slow but steady *swish!* I was not mistaken. It was the one sound in a dark jungle I really dread—the slither of a snake.

Butterflies were fluttering round my stomach and I tried vainly to beat them down. But they would not die because I am cursed with an acute ophidiophobia. Any snake, poisonous or not, fills me with horror. I had to know—even if a light scared the boar away or brought him charging at the hide. I snapped on the spare torch and shone it around the back of my chair. As I moved something sharp drove into my right arm and I sprang up with a stifled cry. But there was nothing there. It was only a prick from a thorn on the duranta, some of which are two inches long.

The snake seemed to have gone. There was no sign of one anywhere near my chair nor under the hedge, and the rustling had stopped, too. But as I settled down again I was still worried. That year the rains had brought snakes out in scores and I was always meeting them in the fields and even in the house. I felt for my pipe and filled it. Some tea would help too, so I groped for the thermos and the little cup on top of it; the hot sweet brew and the strong tobacco steadied me down.

Half an hour later, another noise jerked me up in the chair. It came suddenly, clear and unmistakable: an animal splashing through a puddle left by the rain. Almost at once the splashes gave way to a loud squelching as a heavy body trampled into deep slush. A moment of silence then an abrupt *flop!* as the animal started to wallow in the mud.

It might be a sambur, though more likely the boar. As the safety-catch slipped over, I could hear the animal shaking the mud from its coat. Now it came squelching out of the puddle to the silence of the soft ground and I was left guessing for more than a minute. At last I saw it. A dim black shape ghosting along the game-path towards me.

From my low seat on the ground, it looked as big as a small pony. For a few moments more I was not sure and then I saw the hump of bristles on its neck. Very slowly, I raised the rifle and pointed it towards the boar. But under the shelter of the corrugated sheet there was a black shadow and I couldn't see the end of the barrel; only the blob of the torch mounted near the rear sight. I started to swing with the dark shape on the path as best I could. I should take him when he was right in front of the hide and some fifteen yards off.

He is almost there. My finger has taken the first pressure off the trigger and my left thumb is itching on the switch of the torch. I expect to have about a second after the light goes on to slam the bullet into a vital spot. The boar seems to be creeping, but a few more yards will bring his snout up to the right-hand corner of the hide. . .

. . . *Now!* The torch flicks on and the black bulk on the path bursts into a vivid brown boar bathed in a brilliant circle of light. There's a fleeting glimpse of a gleaming tush and a wicked pink eye glinting in the beam. I see, too, that the bright dot of the foresight is back on his ham. A flick to the left and then a squeeze on the trigger. But even as the rifle roars the boar dips his stern like a speedboat suddenly jabbed to full throttle and a split second later he's out of the beam. And I'm in the dark as the jar of recoil shatters the bulb in the torch.

As the crash of the explosion rocketed away I sprang to my feet, blind after the brilliance of the light. I could hear the boar screaming and threshing about in front of the hide. As I dragged the spare torch from my pocket, I trod on a stick which squashed into the soft ground and then snapped up and slapped against my right boot. I stepped to the left to clear it, but it came too and slapped twice more. I stamped to free it and moved back, but it seemed firmly entangled and thudded against the boot again.

With a final kick I left it. The torch was now in my hand and I smacked it against the forepart of the rifle and clamped it there with my left thumb. I was too late. The boar had found his feet and as the light went on, he was almost in the hide. He was just a big brown blur and I pulled the trigger when the muzzle seemed to be poking him in the snout. The shot didn't stop him—and the next second he crashed through the flimsy screen.

He smashed into my bare knees and knocked me back into the chair which spun over to the sound of splintering wood.

Now there was the wildest confusion. I was hurled around on my knees as his great hairy body and hooves lashed out in all directions. I battered blindly to push away. Then one of the spikes on the duranta drove hard into my leg. The pain was so sudden and intense that it shot me to my feet.

The next moment I had burst out of the hide with the rifle and torch still in my hand. Behind me I could hear the boar staggering over the wreckage. I whipped round, fixed him in the light and fired at his face from three yards. The trigger sagged limply back to the guard. I had neither remembered nor had time to reload.

The boar swayed slightly back and jerked his head to one side as he braced for the charge. In the light, his eyes were a flashing pink and the tushes glinted as he clamped them tight for a running slash. As I bunched my muscles to leap aside, he threw up his head and from the red gash of a bleeding mouth burst a choking roar—half grunt and scream. But the boar stayed where he was, and then I saw him giving at the knees as he started to sink to the ground. I lowered the rifle and snatched back the bolt. As I did the torch swung off him and swept across my overturned chair.

It was just a fleeting glimpse as the light flicked by. But it was quite enough, and in one stunning second the fierce thrill of a fair fight had changed to fluttering fright. All at once I was rooted to the ground even though I could hear the boar still moving. But my eyes and ears were no longer for him. That danger had faded into nothing as I trained the torch and stared at the squirming horror near my chair.

In the bright light, a writhing mass of thick coils were flashing a dirty white and brown. As I stared down, my heart suddenly gave a great leap and an inner voice seemed to be screaming in my ears: *That wasn't the jab of a duranta thorn but the fangs of a snake!*

Almost without knowing what I did I raised the rifle and sent a bullet into that squirming knot. It reared up and then the coils uncurled almost lazily. When it plopped softly back to the grass it lay a thick, twitching brown band.

When the sound of the shot had died away I was conscious of a sudden silence. Vaguely I realized that the boar was dead. Somehow it didn't seem to matter. I was only aware of the snake as I put my hand down to feel the back of my leg just above the knee. My fingers came away covered with blood and for a long moment I stared at them stupidly. At the same time, a sick apprehension was building up inside me as that same little voice whispered in my ear again: *What sort is it?*

As I walked slowly forward, the long narrow beam splashed along the ground tightened to a small white dot of light with the glistening body of the snake strung across its centre. When I was standing right above it, I felt a cold sweat suddenly start to prick out from every pore. Down the length of the light brown body ran three necklaces of black-ringed spots. The mark of the deadly Russell's viper.

I was starting to shiver as I shone the torch on the back of my leg and strained round to look at the wound. At first there was nothing but smeared blood which I wiped away with the hem of my shorts. Then I saw them. Two punctures about half an inch apart. One was more marked than the other and from each ran a jagged line of torn flesh where the fangs had been wrenched away.

Then, as I stared down at those jagged wounds, frightening things started to happen. That cold sweat was soaking my shirt, and I felt a strange tingling seeping through my body and mounting to my brain. Terrifying pictures were starting to flick across the screen of my mind as five words from an old snake book I had at home came back to me. They were from the cold text-book description of an actual case of snake-bite and I could see them so clearly that the printed page might have been under my eyes: *Death followed in sixty-five minutes.*

I knew then that I had to die the way I most dreaded. Home was a long way off and there was nothing I could do to check the poison flowing through my veins. And it was working fast. My breath now was coming in short gasps and my legs were ready to collapse, I fell to the grass and lay still staring up at the stars. All at once they spun into a giddy whirl round the sky and then grew dimmer. With a start I realized that the end was racing on and that I was blacking-out.

Stop it somehow! That little voice was frantic and it jerked me up shaking my head to dispel the fog. Through it, I remembered a tourniquet and slowly started to remove my shirt. When it was off, I tore out some long strips and twisted them together; then I bound my leg just above the wounds and screwed the tourniquet deep into the flesh with a short twig.

The exertion sprang the beading sweat into running streams and left my tongue rasping in a parched mouth. As I swayed back to the grass, the waving torch shone into the wrecked hide. Under the debris in one corner I saw the thermos with the old china cup lying beside it. I crawled over and slopped out some tea. It scalded my throat, but I gulped it all down and felt some strength coming back. After another cup, I struggled up with the determination to get home.

When I was standing up my leg was nearly dead, tingling to a heavy numbness with little feeling when I pinched it. *No feeling.* I looked down and played the light over my knee as I prodded and nipped the flesh. An idea was forming, but it was so frightening that the thought nearly made me sick. In my haversack there was a knife with a razor's edge. I stared at the haversack, doubting. Had I the courage to do what was in my mind and cut the bite out in a deep cone of flesh?

I pulled the haversack towards me and groped for the knife. It was lying at the bottom under a spare pipe and pouch, a tangled pull-through, and a small stove with its box of solid fuel. I shook everything out in front of the light. The hilt of the knife gleamed when I lifted it to slide the blade from its sheath. I felt the edge and even remembered to pour over the blade some of the pure Dettol from the emergency bottle; then I picked up the torch, strained round, and shone the light on the back of my leg.

My heart was pounding fast as I thrashed my dithering courage to plunge the knife in. But I couldn't do it, and the shocking truth was that even in this desperate plight I hadn't got the guts to earn a sporting chance to live. It was the winking blade of the knife when its point was resting so lightly on my skin. The thought was too macabre and ordinary imagination simply could not see it deep in the flesh cutting slowly round the bite.

As I put the knife down I noticed the little white cup lying close to my knee. It was made of thick china and something stirred at the back of my mind. For a few moments I stared at it trying to force I knew not what to the surface. Then it came in a sudden flash. *How Stupid!* I should have done that fifteen minutes ago. A surge of hope bubbled up and I reached for the knife again.

This was not so drastic, and before I could dither again the point sank in and ripped across the flesh in a straight line just above the top puncture. I hardly felt it though the knife had bitten deep. A moment later there was another cut above the fang mark below. After that I picked up the cup and the box of solid fuel. The top cake was already broken into four pieces. I dropped one of these into the cup and felt for matches. The fuel refused to light; it was old and probably damp, but at the fourth try a tiny tongue of blue flame flickered, fizzled stronger, and then leaped into a bluish-yellow flame.

I slapped the cup over the wounds and waited for the burn. It did not come, but just when I thought that the trick was not going to work the suction caught and dragged the flesh into the cup.

It clung like some revolting limpet; then I squeezed the flesh all round the cup trying to force out the poison. The effort was too much; that paralysing weakness swept back and a surging wave of nausea sent me reeling back to the grass. The knife had come too late. The poison had been in my blood for more than twenty minutes. I lay still and stared at the sky as a simple calculation ran through my head: *Twenty from sixty-five leaves forty-five minutes. . .*

. . . *Get home!* The screaming of that little voice smashed through those thoughts and roused a desperate resolve to reach the house. I struggled up on my elbow. The thought of dying here on the sodden ground with nothing but the blackness of the night and the mournful whine of the wind to bow me out was suddenly more than I could bear. With a great effort I staggered to my feet. I was going to get home somehow even though I knew that to arrive would be no reprieve.

There was no antivenene in the house. That was still one of those things 'we really must get', and the nearest centre for proper treatment was at Hoshangabad. That was seventy-odd miles away, inaccessible by road during the rains, impossible reach by rail before three o'clock the next afternoon. . .

I cannot remember all that happened on the way home. But frequent spells of giddiness brought me crashing to the ground, and it was two hours after I started before I staggered out of the night and collapsed on the veranda steps—a grotesque figure in a tattered shirt plastered with black mud from head to foot. In one hand—heaven knows why—I was clutching the dead viper and the cup still clung to my leg, strapped tightly with more strips torn from my shirt.

Now Babs is not frightened of snakes, and when the first shock of my appearance had passed, she began to shake me out of the coma into which I was quickly falling. I believe now that I should not have lasted the night but for her own odd attitude to snakes and the shame she finally stirred in me about 'this nonsense of dying'. For Babs has indeed no fear of snakes and she treats them with such contempt that I regard her behaviour as little short of lunacy. They are either 'big' or 'small' ones, and although she will grudgingly admit that the big ones might be able to harm you, the small ones are just too absurd for words and always 'squiggle away when you approach'.

However, that night she might have been wiser than I knew, for her cure was undoubtedly effective. And she began it by dismissing the viper lightly, after a single glance, as 'not so very big after all'. Then, while my wounds were being swabbed with antiseptic, she kept up a fatuous running commentary on why such a 'baby one' couldn't kill me. I was in no mood to argue and it is as well that I didn't; for although I knew that all the twaddle she put across was based on a light-hearted refusal to realize the risks, her own confidence was so real that in the end, it undoubtedly restored mine enough to believe that a chance still existed.

With the first part of the cure over she next brewed—having once been an army wife—a steaming potion of that old panacea which all soldiers know as a cure for every ill from a rough slice of the sergeant's tongue to a fatal wound—'ot sweet tea'.

That night it justified its reputation; for at the end of another hour I was not only still alive but had to admit that I felt 'not too bad'. Nor did I, when I really analysed my feelings. The cold sweat had gone and I could move my limbs normally, and the throbbing about my leg felt like nothing more than the results of my own crude surgery. And now, for the first time, I realized that the searing agony of the poison which ought to have been dominating all else, just was not there—nor had it ever been.

Yet, there was not the slightest doubt that the snake was a Russell's viper and one of the most poisonous we have. Something, it seemed, had gone wrong and for some reason I didn't yet know, little or no poison had been injected by the fangs. I began to think back to those confused moments in the hide after I had fired at the boar.

I, of course, knew now that some time before the shot, the viper had wormed into the warmth of the hide and was near my feet when I sprang up. When I stamped on its body, I mistook it for an 'up-ending' bit of stick. The viper certainly struck at my boot four times, and there were perhaps other strikes I did not feel. Almost immediately after this, the boar came charging in and at least two other things could have happened in the fracas. The viper might have bitten the boar and perhaps more than once as he rolled on the ground; and it was a fact that something had trodden on the viper's head, though there was nothing to show whether it was boot or hoof. This alone might have forced every drop of poison from the sacs, if indeed there was any left after the strikes at my boot, and perhaps a bite or two at the boar. I got the last bite of all; and even then, before the fangs drove in, they had passed through two folds of my shorts.

These theories were nice and comforting, and I was now sure that because of one or all of them I was not going to die. Nevertheless, I was still puzzled. What about that cold sweat? And what about the loss of power in my limbs and the other symptoms of snake-bite? Those had been very real and not imagination. Indeed, merely remembering them brought back a shudder, and mixed well into that memory were those 'sixty-five minutes'.

On a shelf at the end of the room was the book those words came from: *Poisonous Terrestrial Snakes* by Major F. Wall, I.M.S., C.M.Z.S. It is an excellent work, and although written many years ago it is still an authority. I turned first to the bit about 'death in sixty-five minutes' and found that I had been worrying about the wrong snake. Those words referred to the bite from a cobra whose venom is more virulent, and in lethal doses quicker, than that of the Russell's viper. I, then, thumbed to the general remarks on snake-bite poisoning and got perhaps the biggest shock that night.

I had indeed been on the very threshold of death and but for the kindly hand of fate I could have made the crossing, cobra or not, within sixty-five minutes. There had been nothing false about those symptoms and they could have ended my life. And if I had died I should have killed myself *with sheer blue funk!*

Listen to what Wall's book has to say:

'Now in cases of snake-bite, whether the wounds are inflicted by a harmless or a poisonous species, a certain train of symptoms follow which are the direct result of fright and kindred emotions . . . the symptoms of fright often very speedily declare themselves, far more speedily than is ever the case in snake poisoning. . . Some of these are so serious that they end fatally. To take examples. . . A fatality from the bite of a "bis cobra", one of the monitor lizards (probably *Varanus bengalensis*). The subject was a woman of fifty who was bitten on the toe, and she died in 1½ hours. I believe there is not the slightest doubt that this lizard is completely innocuous. . . The death of a woman in Ceylon from the bite of a common wolf-snake (*Lycodon auliculis*) a perfectly harmless species . . . all of which was due to fright. . . A man came under my care in Rangoon in an unconscious state having been bitten by a harmless water snake . . . was unconscious 17 hours. . .'

I was scaring myself to death. That was the sorry truth, and if there is any moral in this story it lies here. For I might have recalled, had I really tried, something much more cheerful than those sixty-five minutes from the same book. This, prominent in italics: *That it is quite possible to be bitten by a poisonous snake without being poisoned.*

THE LONELY TIGER

'Times have changed.'

Along one shelf in our library are the books on shikar that helped to bring me to Mandikhera. They go back to 1858, exactly a hundred years, and in most of them that phrase crops up repeatedly. Nearly all the writers use it, and with few exceptions, they use it before going on to lament the growing scarcity of game.

A lot certainly has changed in the last hundred years and the game has indeed grown steadily scarcer. Just how much scarcer is shown strikingly between the first book on the shelf and the last. In the first, published during the Mutiny, the author was a Lieut. William Rice, who tells of shooting ninety-eight tigers, four leopards and twenty-five bears during one hot weather furlough. In the last book, on a shoot of about the same length of time, the writer admits he was lucky and well content with two tigers and one leopard.

The books written in the decade or so following the Mutiny show the gradual changes as they came. One of the main changes was brought about by the swift and terrible punishment meted out for the revolt. When that was over and the stick finally hung behind the door, it was at last safe for sportsmen to wander even in the remotest jungles. That, perhaps, was the golden age of Indian shikar: the animals were in their hundreds, and although the only weapon was still the muzzle-loader, the slaughter was incredible. Then, as the ramrod and powder-horn gave way to the breech-loader and the magazine rifle, some of the old ideas of sport started to change, too. Game was still plentiful, but some sportsmen now began to realize that it might not last forever, if weapons became even handier and more powerful.

Not much later, every serious writer was a little worried. The animals really *were* being thinned down. There was of course still plenty of sport, but now come the first pleas to make it last and the first criticisms of the over keen sports men that never knew when they'd had enough. Another menace these writers noted was the growing number of 'native gunners over waterholes', and they suggested a drastic curtailment of the muzzle-loaders allowed for crop protection.

Towards the closing years of British rule in India, there was real concern for the game. A lot of animals now were scarce and some kinds of them already well along the road to extinction. Even so, few of these later writers considered the position hopeless and most agreed about what should be done to improve it. A tightening of forest rules and stricter enforcement, a low limit to any individual's bag, more and larger game sanctuaries and—above all else—much more plain common sense.

Sound enough. In some other countries where the animals had been hunted as hard as they had been in India, prompt and energetic action had not only saved most of the game but seen it increase. The same thing would work here.

Then it was 1947, and with Independence times really *did* change. Old-time sportsmen, had they seen it, would have been speechless with amazement, for almost overnight an entirely new kind of hunter had started to roam the jungles. There had of course been black sheep before, but most hunters had obeyed the rules and shot in conventional ways. Not so the new men. Forest rules for them just did not exist and they shot neither on foot nor from a machan. Instead, they rode in a jeep, and as it sneaked along forest roads at night they picked off everything that showed up in the headlights from the comfort and security of the front seat.

At much the same time, the old 'water-hole gunner' really came into his own. The satanic government that had imposed those harsh measures to keep muzzle-loaders and 12-bores out of irresponsible hands, was gone. Now, almost anyone that cared to apply for a licence, was sure to get one. In no time at all, freshly killed venison was on display in the bazaars.

Indian sportsmen were aghast, and their letters of protest were soon flooding into newspaper offices. But they did little good; these sportsmen were a tiny minority and nothing they said or tried to do made the slightest difference: they were cranks from the bad old days.

This change came fast and its effects were noticeable almost at once. Indeed, looking back now it seems as though the animals disappeared overnight. All of them, of course, had not been shot. It was just that they were not seen about so often, and when they were seen, there was something about the way they fled that showed them sensible of the constant threat now abroad both by day and night.

It was not like this ten years ago. Then, herds of chital and nilgai were a common sight on any dawn round of the estate. Sambur would be about too if you were early enough and in the right place, and there was hardly a morning that showed no glimpse of barking deer and four-horned antelope and the dainty chinkara sporting about the more open ravines.

Then the shots started to echo through the nights. Most of them were the long-drawn-out *Boo-o-oom!* of muzzle-loaders using the always-slightly-damp bazaar black powder. For the first few nights I believed it was just a sudden increase in the occasional poaching that has always worried us. But when the shots continued night after night, it was obvious that something unusual was going on.

A few inquiries soon showed what was happening. A lot of the small cultivators around us had acquired guns 'to protect their fields'. But they were not sitting over their crops. After dark most of them were roaming the forests in bullock-carts and shooting at any animal they met by the light of a torch. Along the main road that runs two miles from the estate, matters were even worse. At night this road is used by a lot of animals which come out of the jungle on each side of it. Now, after them, went trucks and private cars creeping along in low gear with headlights blazing and a spot sweeping the sides—and perhaps as many as four gunners ready for the first pair of eyes to flash back at the lights.

These mechanized rogues had better weapons, shotguns with a sprinkling of old rifles. With these, the kills came easily. So did the money for skins, meat and horns. This was too much for the passengers in the local buses: such easy money could not be ignored and so these, too, began taking their weapons in case anything showed up along the way. Something often did, and then an obliging driver—for a hunk of meat—would stop the bus and allow the shot to be taken through the window.

Most of the sportsmen that saw what was going on sent in reports. At first, though, they were not really worried for something like this was bound to happen when the old ban on firearms was suddenly lifted. Such flagrant poaching would of course not be allowed to go on; just let a few offenders be fined and have their arms confiscated and the abuses would stop. The authorities, when reports reached them, were bound to act quickly.

That the authorities did nothing was perhaps the biggest shock of all. The slaughter went on and there was not the slightest evidence that anything was being done to stop it. Nobody seemed to care, and as things got worse *The Times of India* came out with this:

'The Uttar Pradesh conference on the preservation of wild life has very appropriately drawn the country's attention to the depredations of poachers and trigger-happy shikaris. Herds of chital, chinkara and spotted deer have become rare and the reason for this, according to U.P.'s chief game warden, is the use of buckshot by shikaris who fire into a herd. For every animal that is killed on the spot, several others are injured by buckshot, and these beasts suffer a slow death from festering wounds. In parts of Uttar Pradesh poaching has apparently become organized business: in some towns of Lakhimpur Kheri district people seldom buy mutton; they prefer venison which is cheaper and readily available in the bazaar thanks to the very private enterprise of the poachers. Professional bird catchers are playing havoc with winged fauna and the conference was told that partridge and quail are on the verge of extinction. The Uttar Pradesh Government can be expected to accept the conference's recommendation that a two-year ban be imposed on the use of buck-shot and that the U.P. Birds and Wild Animals Protection Act be amended to put an end to the malpractices of the professional bird catchers. But this will not be enough.

Strengthening the law is no substitute for enforcing what is already on the statute book, and the conference revealed that the enforcement aspect has been neglected to an incredible extent. What is one to make of the official admission that a large number of poachers are Government servants? It is fair to assume that what is true of Uttar Pradesh is more or less true of other States. Government officials attending the Naini tal conference were unable to suggest steps to put an end to this deplorable state of affairs. Divisional Commissioners and other senior revenue and police officials have promised to dissuade their subordinates from poaching, but persuasion is a curious method of enforcing the law.'

Right from the start, the poachers on our own land became an unmitigated nuisance. Very early on they got Leggy, a four-horned antelope, who screamed home one morning with a back leg hanging from a sinew after a meeting with a sneaking bullock-cart in the big nullah. Not long after, they got Sammy. He was a barking deer and you will hear more about him in the next chapter.

I saw some of the tragedy that was now getting into its stride from my wooden armchair above the pool in the nullah. This chair is built permanently into the fork of a giant tree and has been there nearly ten years. It is thirty feet above the pool and commands wide sweeps of the jungle beyond both banks. I use it a lot throughout the year and often spend whole nights in it watching the animals coming down to drink. The best time is towards the end of the hot weather. By then, the other pools in the nullah have dried up and this one holds the only water for a long way around.

The first hot weather after the change brought some of the tragedy now going on after dark into sharp focus. That year the mowha flowers were late. When at last they started to fall from hundreds of trees in a long strip of jungle near the pool, that was the only water for a considerable distance. At once, that strip became a death trap. The sweet fleshy petals of these flowers draw herbivorous animals like a magnet, and when the sickly sweet scent brought them to the strip, the bullock-carts were waiting in the darkness under the trees and on the road through it were the crawling trucks and jeeps.

The deer and antelopes were the hardest hit and brought to the pool the saddest stories of all. I would see fawns, which had been with their mothers a short time before suddenly appear alone, their eyes big and frightened in the moonlight; or a frantic hind, mad with anxiety, would come dashing down to the water searching desperately for a baby which would never nestle into her side again.

Nothing was being spared, and for every animal killed outright, several more got away wounded. Some of these staggered to the pool at their last gasp for a last drink. Others, not so badly hit, would come trembling with terror to quench a burning thirst. After doing that they would limp painfully away—perhaps to weeks of agony unless they were found and destroyed in the morning. For no shot is ever fired from the chair; the pool is a sanctuary and I like to believe that the animals know it.

It was late one night when I first saw the cub. He seemed to have come to the pool alone although he was obviously a very young tiger. By now, however, that was nothing unusual and he was very likely searching for a mother he would never find. Under the hard light of a full moon, I watched him flitting about by the water's edge. He seemed quite happy, and if his solitary state concerned him he was not showing it. He was not thirsty either for he made no attempt to drink but just played with the dead leaves rustling on the sand in the light breeze.

I was just wondering how to catch him in the morning when his mother materialized from the shadows under the left bank of the nullah. As she came, another cub was playing with her tail. She went straight to the pool and drank, then the three glided away as silently as they had come.

The next evening, I was up in the chair early. The night before, those cubs had looked young enough for that outing to have been one of their first. If that was true, it suggested a hideout close to the pool and the tigress would certainly come again. But as the moon was bright and she would come up warily, I had taken Bimbo with me and tied him in the branches above my head.

Bimbo is a langur monkey who hates all the big cats. For this reason, he often earns his keep because the merest glimpse of a tiger or leopard sets him screaming his lungs out and dancing about the tree like a drunken dervish. That kind of performance is often useful to put a suspicious animal at ease if it has either seen or heard anything unusual from where you are sitting. But once Bimbo starts his act there can be no doubt—it was only a monkey after all.

The tigress came soon after nine o'clock and Bimbo was off the moment she appeared. But this time it didn't work for when the tigress looked up she must have spotted me at once. She did not come to the pool again for more than two months; rather than expose her cubs to a possible risk she drank at the river some way to the south. It was on a night much later when I did not expect them that the three glided down to the pool again. That was the last time I saw the tigress alive. When I saw her next, she was stretched on the concrete floor of a garage twenty miles away. A truck driver had shot her the previous night.

■

When I found the tigress in the garage I was on my way to Jubbulpore for three days. Had it been possible to skip my appointment I should have gone straight back to look for the cubs. As it was, I could only wonder what had become of them all the time I was away. If they had been close to their mother when she was killed either of two fates could have overtaken them: they might have been shot or captured. The last possibility was the more likely. Tiger cubs are a rich prize and they are not difficult to round up because all young animals suddenly losing mothers will hang about the spot where she disappeared from for several days.

Those cubs had been so much on my mind that I went down to the pool shortly after I got home and began to search along the water's edge. I was not really expecting to find any sign of them, but almost at once I found their small pug marks and near them, half buried in the sand, a chewed peacock's feather with traces of blood. An hour later, I had found more feathers and the remains of a full-grown peacock.

The cubs were safe after all and obviously needed no help from me. The wily peacock is difficult to surprise, and to have got one, the cubs must already be using 'big tiger' tactics and haunting the game-paths leading to the water. They could safely be left on their own, but to keep an eye on them I meant to find their hideout.

It was a good place. The tigress had chosen well and was rearing them in a deep cave with a narrow slit of an entrance well screened with thorns on the side of a hill. It was, as I had suspected, not far from the pool; yet I might never have found it but for the lucky accident of seeing, from some high ground a little way off, one of the cubs coming out.

Once I knew where they lived, I got to know them well with glasses from that high ground. They grew fast, and it was not long before they were hunting bigger game; nor was it long before they were roaming farther afield. Then they started staying away from the cave for days at a time. I was sorry about that; they had been a source of endless delight and this meant that they would not be staying much longer for they were now big enough to split up.

At last, I thought they had gone. More than a week went by and there had been no sign of them near the cave. But most evenings I climbed to the high ground and searched with the glasses. Then one evening they were back and I knew that they had killed something near the entrance to the cave. The clue was vultures waiting patiently on a silk-cotton tree half-way up the hill.

I enjoy stalking, so I set off to get near enough to watch them on whatever they had killed. After some time, I picked up the young tigress lying on some grass in a patch of shade. But of the tiger and the kill there was no sign, although I spent another fifteen minutes looking round for them.

I was just starting to turn back when I felt that something was wrong. For a few seconds I thought that sixth sense was warning of danger; the tiger now was big enough to be rough if he caught me near his kill. Before moving, I glanced all round me and then climbed higher up the hill. There was still no sign of him, but from my new position I saw on the ground below me some vultures I had not noticed before. A moment later I realized the truth. There was no kill and the vultures were hopping slowly towards the tigress because she was dead.

Her body was still warm. She could not have died much more than an hour before. Her white stomach, still bearing traces of her baby-coat, was swollen and had been punctured by buckshot in a tightly grouped pattern. The grass all around had been flattened by her final struggles; her lips were drawn back in a snarl of pain hurled at the last cruel agonies of a lingering death.

Where was the tiger? Was he, too, either dead or dying of wounds somewhere near the cave? It was not unlikely. The cubs would almost certainly have been met together, and if they had been met with dazzling headlights, the glare would have 'fixed' them long enough for the second barrel. I searched until dark but couldn't find him.

Early the next morning I knew that he was not dead. He had drunk at the pool during the night, and when I saw the vultures keeping to the trees, I knew that he was lying somewhere close to the dead tigress.

Soon after lunch, I was up in the chair above the pool. The day was warm enough to send the tiger to drink early. But in case he was late, I had mounted a torch on a rifle. Yes, I was going to break the no-shooting-from-the-chair rule if he showed any signs of a wound serious enough either to kill him after days of agony or leave him so crippled that his life would be a misery and perhaps a danger to man and beast.

The afternoon was indeed hot and drowsy and I am ashamed to admit that the droning jungle soon lulled me to sleep. It was five-thirty before I finally struggled out of warm hazy dreams and with a sudden start saw the tiger on the far side of the water.

Fortunately he missed the startled movement as I woke for he was looking away as he lay on the sand by the water's edge. When the sleep was off my eyes I saw that he was staring intently at a leaf blowing over the surface and drifting towards him. When it came within reach he started to dab at it with his right front paw, but with a touch so gentle that his pad was the merest caress on the tiny tip of its curled-up sail. From that moment, I always called him the Lonely Tiger. His expression was so forlorn that there flashed into my mind the vision of a small boy pondering the cruel fate that had killed first his mother and then his sister, and so condemned him to the heartache of loneliness and unexciting games played on his own.

All at once he smashed his little boat into the water with a sudden splash. *Just a silly kid's game!* Then before I quite realized what he was doing he had reminded me why I was at the pool by starting to lick at his left front paw. From my perch thirty feet above him I saw it at once: a small patch of red flesh licked clean of fur. I leant forward to watch. But he licked nowhere else so that seemed the only wound he had. I wondered whether it would be just a single pellet from the second barrel.

I waited till he got to his feet and started down the nullah. He went slowly and with a limp, but the wound in his paw still seemed to be the only injury he had. I let him go; from that he would recover with few or no ill effects.

He was to limp for the rest of his life. On wet sand and damp earth which held the impressions of pug marks well, the left front paw always showed a little twisted with the outside toe pressing deeper than the others. This was to tell me in the years to come when the Lonely Tiger had been round. . .

■

The tiger never used the cave again and many months passed without a sign of him. Then he came back, but now he was only a casual caller because he had settled down on a regular 'beat' which took him about ten days to get round. The wound in his paw evidently had healed well and he seemed a normal tiger living on jungle game, for no report of a cattle-kill ever came in when he was about.

Some time later, he disappeared completely for nearly a year. Where he went I never knew, but it was most likely a wife that kept him away from his old haunts; when they finally called him back, he probably left a family in some distant jungle.

When at last that familiar pug mark appeared in the nullah again it was like an unexpected visiting card from an old friend. Once more he had come back to settle down on a beat, so whenever he was expected I started to sit over the pool for I badly wanted to see what he looked like now.

He came at last on a night when there was no moon. But even a tiger cannot pass silently over dry leaves and I heard him crunching across the thick carpet of them I had spread on the nullah bed. When the torch flicked on he stopped dead and stared back at the beam. He was a magnificent animal, his coat glossy and but lightly marked with stripes. The light held him for more than a minute before he started to edge away. That night I should have taught him a lesson, a shot near his nose then might have given this story a different ending. But neither I nor the Lonely Tiger knew then that the sands of his life were running out and that he had only eight more days to live. . .

For the past two weeks, I had been hearing a great deal

about the man shooting in the block a few miles to the north. 'One of the richest men of all, sahib,' Bhutu told me. Certainly something unusual was going on. From all accounts the camp arrangements were fantastic: luxuries galore and enough servants to astonish an old-time Viceroy. But in spite of the luxuries, hundreds of beaters, and a dozen or more young buffaloes for baits, no tiger had been shot up to the beginning of the third week.

I thought I knew what was going on. Since Independence, there have sprung up in India firms to deal with visiting sportsmen from overseas. A few of these are excellent and they do their clients well; they also observe all the forest rules and make sure that animals are shot by fair means. There are other firms not so good and some that should not be allowed to operate at all. These last ones are interested in nothing but money and if they know the forest rules they seldom obey them; and as their hunting experience is usually nil, their safest bet to get trophies is to allow their clients to shoot from jeeps.

The camp I had been hearing about was a show run by perhaps the worst of the bad firms. When this shoot was nearing its end, I happened to meet the client casually one day on the road. He hailed from some country 'south of the border' and spoke English with a strong American accent. He was very disgruntled about no tiger, for he had just come from Africa where animals 'grow on every bush'. On parting he asked me if I could sell him a tiger skin, in the event of his shoot ending with no tiger in the bag.

But the shoot was not yet over. If it had started slowly, this probably was only because the man in charge of it had no intention of making things appear too easy. He had charged a great deal of money, and it was therefore necessary at first to make some show of getting a tiger by normal hunting methods. From what I heard the attempts had been pretty pathetic; so now, with the shoot drawing to an end, it was time to start using the jeeps at night.

They got him on the fourth night. The jeep had left camp soon after midnight for the best time was 'towards morning'. On this trip tiger again was top priority, but if anything else showed up it was not to be neglected. Nor was it. Twenty minutes after the start, an immature sambur stag fell to a .375 magnum. It was covered with leaves and left where it dropped to be collected in the morning for it was too early yet to clutter the rack at the back of the jeep: 'You just never could tell when you might want the room.' Wise counsel as it turned out, for later the rack held a chital hind.

By now time was getting on. But the night was not yet over, and just a little farther along the road another victim was waiting. As the first fingers of dawn reached up for the sky, his brilliant eyes blazed back at the headlights. For a few seconds the animal was indistinct. Then the jeep was juddering to a crawl as the guide pointed excitedly ahead with *There he is!*

A tiger stood across the road. As the jeep purred nearer, it sounded no note of danger. His puckered mask held only a puzzled expression as the bright eyes stared at the oncoming lights. The jeep closed to a few yards. The tiger at last turned slowly towards the side of the road. As he moved, the bullet smacked into his belly, low and far back.

The tearing pain of the bullet kept him moving for almost a mile. Then the shock brought him down beside a patch of thorns. He was mortally wounded and in terrible agony. Left alone he would have gone no farther; but the first grey of dawn had now changed to lemon-coloured light and through it he saw two men, still some distance away, moving along his trail. He staggered away without being seen and then rested again where the jungle borders Bhutu's field on the northern boundary of the estate.

At dawn that morning, I was not far away from this boundary with Bhutu and two other men helping to stamp out the last smoldering patches of a fire which had burnt all night. We heard Bhutu's wife shouting long before she reached us with the news that a tiger had just crossed their field and had growled when it saw her.

We found the two men first. They were examining a fresh patch of blood under a tree. One was armed with an old single barrel 12-bore, the other had an axe. When I had found out who they were, they readily told the whole story and then amazed me more by explaining how they had been left behind 'to find the dead tiger'. The rest, with One-Shot Sam, had gone comfortably home to a hearty breakfast.

When the men were forbidden to search farther, the one with the gun started to argue. The tiger, he said, had to be found. The foreign burra sahib badly wanted the skin and would make trouble if he didn't get it. I sent Bhutu and Jaganath to see them on their way and to make sure that they did not slip back.

When I started to follow the blood trail, I was still unaware that I was after the Lonely Tiger. He ought to have been miles away on his beat for he was not due back for another two or three days. But where the trail left the leafy carpet of the forest for a path through scrub, I suddenly found that twisted pug clearly printed in the fine dust. This, although a shock, was also a help. A strange tiger would have been making off at random and any cover that offered the slightest security might have concealed it. But not this one. At least I was ready to bet that when thinking of a safe place to hide he would be making for the cave.

The trail was easy to follow. The tiger, still losing blood, had kept to a path which winds diagonally across the side of a wooded hill. Near the bottom of this the path forks, the right branch curling down to the nullah, the other going on over boulder-strewn ground under heavy jungle to the tiger's old cave. The blood turned away to the right. My guess had been wrong, but once that idea had been tossed out of my mind I realized that the pool in the nullah was the obvious place for the tiger to make for. What he must need now more than anything else was water.

I should find him by the pool. That was certain; for he had been forced to rest at two places on the way down from the top of the hill and that had slowed him up considerably; now, he could not be very far ahead. From the fork, I crept to within fifty yards of the nullah and then left the path to make a detour through the jungle which would bring me out above the pool from a flank.

I regretted doing this at once. The noise of my progress now was dangerous. The surface of the path had been powder-soft and dead silent, but the ground here was strewn with dry leaves and I seemed to be treading on them all. There was no time to go back. Having once started it was best to keep going as quietly as I could and make for a screen of bushes ahead that edged the bank just above the pool. At last I reached them and paused briefly; then I inched forward the last two yards and looked down at the pool.

The nullah bed was empty. One quick sweeping glance took it all in. Then a sudden chill swept through me when I saw what I had walked into. The water in the pool was cloudy with slow swirls of muddy sediment still settling to the bottom. The tiger had only just left. Across the dry sand, I could see the deep pocks left by his pugs still ringed with a thin wet line. The tracks led from the water to where the path sloped up the bank . . . the path I had just left.

There could be little doubt that he had heard me coming. But now, instead of running away, he had turned to meet the threat and had come up the path to fight. From somewhere very close he was watching me. I kept quite still, ears straining, eyes searching frantically for some sign: the attack might come at any second—the only warning a sudden noisy charge over the dry leaves from wherever he was hiding.

I saw him first from the corner of my eye. He was crouched by a teak tree twenty yards off and a little behind me. The next second, the foresight was racing towards him.

But I was too late. Death was staring straight back at me from the tiger's eyes even as I swung towards him. As I stared back, I heard the pounding of my heart and the frantic cries of monkeys which had just spotted him from the trees along the nullah. They were very excited. But then they didn't know as I did that the Lonely Tiger was dead.

MIDNIGHT ENCOUNTER

I started this book by saying that a walking stick was an adequate weapon for most strolls through the jungle. That of course was before 'times had changed' and before I had met any of the wounded animals I was to come across later. Now I seldom go far without a rifle, and this story is one of the first reasons that changed my mind.

It was a dark night, and only when the tail light of the bus was winking to a red pinpoint way up the road did I remember my torch on the front seat. I had just returned from Jubbulpore a day earlier than Babs expected me, and when I got off at Matkuli there was a two-mile walk through the jungle to get home. When I set off, it was just after eleven o'clock and there was no reason to expect anything else but a pleasant stroll through the dark night. The village street was deserted as most people were already in bed, but half-way down it I found Behari loading his cart with grain for an early start to market. For a few minutes I stopped to chat, and when he knew that I was walking home without a light he offered me a lantern and an axe. I accepted both gratefully; a light would keep me to the track and the little jungle axes make comfortable walking-sticks.

Just beyond the village, the track wanders through fairly

open country. When I was crossing this, the night was not too dark as the bright stars showed a few yards of the track ahead before it was bitten off by the night. But after I had gone a mile, the black mass of the jungle loomed up against the dark sky and when I came under the trees I could see nothing. The lantern was almost useless; it had probably never been cleaned in its life and the flickering flame was striving to show 'through a glass darkly'.

For a few hundred yards I trudged on with my footsteps a series of muffled crunches on the sandy track. Then I startled the first wild creature. From somewhere over to my right came the sharp alarm call of a barking deer, a warning taken up almost at once by a chital hind farther away. The behaviour of wild animals always interests me and so I stopped, wondering whether anything else would answer the chital. Nothing did, but the call of the barking deer came twice more, each time a little nearer than the first.

I couldn't be sure, but that coming nearer suggested that something was wrong and that the deer was frightened of something more dangerous than I was. The wind said that, for it was blowing from behind me and almost straight to the deer.

My scent must have been strong in its nostrils. Yet still it came on and called once more. I stood waiting and undecided. Deer sometimes seek the protection of man against the big cats, but there was something else I suspected as well. I stepped off the track and began tramping noisily through the fallen leaves and swinging the lantern high. When I had gone some fifty yards and the wind was full on my back and blowing straight towards where I judged the deer to be, I stopped. Then I gave a low whistle and the sharp bark of the muntjac. Nothing happened for two minutes; then, hesitantly, a faint rustling from not far away. Slowly the rustling came nearer, an animal tiptoeing through the leaves. For the last few paces it came with a rush and broke into the circle of light thrown by the lantern. A young barking deer, its horns just beginning to sprout.

'What goes on, fathead?' I asked it. 'Can't look after yourself even in your own jungles, eh?'

This was Sammy, and we'd had him since he was a few hours old. The men who had brought him said that his mother had abandoned him in the jungle. That may or may not have been true: those men were poachers and it was more likely that Sammy's mother had disappeared into their cooking pots. Sammy, then, was the merest slip of a 'Disney' fawn, all long spindly legs and soft fluffy ears. In spite of this, he thrived from the first day on a baby's bottle. He took to it like an experienced infant, and the only real difficulty we ever had about his meals was to persuade him that he'd had enough. For the first few months he was content to wander near the house; but as he grew older he started to roam farther afield. We seldom tried to restrain him unless we knew it was more unsafe than usual for him to be out.

On this night when I met Sammy, he had been wandering the jungles after dark for several months. By daybreak he was always back, usually bedded down somewhere near the front veranda preparing to sleep. However, the time now was just a few minutes to midnight and something on the prowl had obviously alarmed him as I was coming up. So, whether he liked the idea or not, the safest place for him was home. Sammy submitted meekly while I tied one end of a scarf round his neck, and when we set off to rejoin the track he trotted along quite willingly close to my side.

We had gone perhaps a hundred yards when he stopped suddenly and brought me up with a sharp tug on the scarf. As I could not pull him on without hurting his neck I stepped back to shove him on from behind. When I touched him he was trembling, and he came in close to my knees, pressing hard against them. He kept his head high in the air while his dilated nostrils sniffed the wind and his eyes stared over to our left. I straightened up and began to listen. There was nothing but the cicadas and the soft rustle of the wind through the trees. At last I managed to urge him on; but his gait now was like some crude marionette, jerky and stiff, his head held woodenly erect and still staring to the left.

All at once I heard it. Just the faintest rustle of dry leaves from behind us and to the left. Impossible to know what it was, and the only thing I could do was to go on pushing Sammy along the track towards home. I suspected a leopard, one of the bold ones not much scared of a light and thoroughly familiar with man. I raised the lantern as high as I could and waved it about. The rustling didn't come again and I went on pushing Sammy home.

I was just thinking that Sammy's nose must have played him false, when the most alarming noises broke out only a few yards to our left. With a sudden loud crashing, some large animal started to force a way through heavy brush. That lasted only a few seconds and then whatever it was began to thresh madly about as though engaged in some high-spirited frolic.

As the noise went on I realized what it was. Not a leopard but a bear, though what the fool was doing only another bear would know. But even with a bear it was safer to clear out fast, he's a jungle clod far better left alone even when he seems on his best behaviour. I lowered the lantern almost to the ground and tried to make Sammy quicken his pace. But he was still reluctant to move along the track and dug in his small pointed hooves as I shoved him on from behind.

It was difficult to move him, and after some moments of hard shoving I was sweating and getting rather bad-tempered. All at once I stopped. Why waste so much energy? Our leopard had turned out to be a bear, and even that—as far as I could tell now—had gone away. But even if it was still about, it would not hurt Sammy and so he could be left to take his usual chance in the jungle. As I bent to untie the knot in the scarf, he was still trembling and every sinew under the twitching flesh was strung tight. I tried to calm him down, stroking his back and caressing his ears. He took no notice: his neck stayed stiff and he kept his eyes staring straight ahead. Then, without warning, he reared back and nearly jerked the scarf from my hand. A second later, he yapped his sharp bark of alarm.

Now he was tugging so violently that I was wrenched right round. For a few moments I fought him, then something made me turn my head and look over my shoulder. In the light of the lamp, I saw a vague form lying across the track. It was only a few yards from us and I whipped up the lantern to see it better. It was a leopard.

Sammy saved us, for even as I stared the front paws teetered as it steadied to spring. Then the scarf snapped tight and I was wrenched back, as the leopard left the ground.

It is not easy to describe something that caught you unawares and then happened in the twinkling of an eye. But even though I had been pulled out of the way, my immediate impression was that the leopard had missed us deliberately. Stranger still, when the leopard hit the ground he seemed to have lost control and hurtled out of the light in a great burst of sand and flying leaves. The next instant that mad threshing started again. It was as though the leopard had been gripped by some terrible anger and was tearing wildly at everything within reach. Those furious sounds were now coming from behind us and they suddenly goaded Sammy to life.

All at once he was off, racing for home as fast as his legs could carry him. So was I. The end of the scarf was still in my hand and it seemed the best idea in the world to be flying from that crazy brute in the bushes. Only when we came to our long drive at the end of the jungle did we slacken speed. Then, panting for breath, we went more slowly until we reached the house. Once there, I took Sammy across to the cowsheds and bundled him in with the calves. He went willingly, with none of the prancing nonsense he usually put on whenever we shut him up for his own good.

While Babs boiled some coffee and made sandwiches, I was thinking about that curious leopard. I was still shaken, but the more I thought about what had happened the more I realized how very odd the whole incident had been. It was altogether *too* odd to be dismissed as just a lucky escape. Something was wrong, and so wrong that it could not be left as it was because strange happenings like this often lead to trouble.

At that moment, I could think of no explanation to fit all the facts. Indeed, the only thing I was sure of was that leopards just do *not* behave as the one we had recently met; and to have seen it at all was perhaps the most perplexing aspect of the whole affair. As a general rule the leopard wears an invisible cloak, an annoying fact that accounts for a great deal of its success.

By the time the coffee and sandwiches were finished, I had decided to go out again. I changed into a pair of light rubber shoes and put new batteries in the spare torch and into the one mounted on a rifle. In case these preparations should give the idea that I was solemnly setting out to stalk a leopard through a black jungle strewn with crackling leaves, let me add quickly that was not my intention at all. The theory I had formed by now was that this leopard was dangerous because it was desperate. It had probably been wounded, and on account of that was so hungry that it was prepared to take risks to get a meal. If that was true there was a fair chance that it was still about; and if it was and still making all that noise it should be possible to locate it before it found me.

That's not so brave as it sounds. This time I should be accompanied by the three dogs and not by a frightened deer. These were odds no leopard would ever take on. If it found us first, there was no doubt it would bow to a superior force and make off.

We set off briskly along the drive. When we came to the end of it we slowed, and a hundred yards into the jungle beyond we stopped to listen. We were showing no lights, so the blackness around was intense and alive with the noise of millions of insects. Somewhere to our left I heard monkeys in a tree; their sentinels had seen us and made us out for what we were, now they were passing us on as friends to their brothers round about by rustling the branches. They had a message for us, too: the leopard was not near us and so we could go on slowly towards where I had left him.

Our eyes were getting more used to the darkness. Now, for a few yards ahead, the track was dimly visible and on each side of it the faint outlines of trees. On the soft sand, trodden free of dead leaves, we were creeping along without a sound. After ten minutes, we stopped to listen again. There was nothing to hear, and this time there were no monkeys near us. That was a pity as we were getting close to the scene of my recent encounter. After another fifty yards I stopped suddenly, when a sound ahead caught my ears.

It had come from not far away and to our left, and, from the sounds that had followed the first, there was little doubt that we had found the leopard. But the noise it was making now was more puzzling than ever. That mad threshing had stopped, and in its place was a light muffled thumping with an irregular rhythm. As I listened I knew that the unlikely had happened, we had found the leopard first and he still knew nothing about us. Once more we crept quietly forward. A few steps now would bring us into the ideal night range of about forty yards. At my heels I could sense the excitement mounting in the dogs; they could scent the quarry for what it was and were waiting eagerly for the shot.

Soon we were as close as I thought we could safely get. But before switching on the torch, I tried to place the leopard exactly by the noise it was making. In front of me I could see the black mass of some bushes, and if the noise was an indication the leopard was under them. I raised the rifle and pressed the switch on the torch.

The light blazed and lit up a large clump of thorns. It was much denser than I expected and there was no sign of the leopard. I kept the torch on and played the beam quickly over the thorns. All the time I was expecting the leopard to take some violent action. But nothing happened. The leopard took not the slightest notice of the light and just went on with that *thump! . . . thump! thump! . . . thump!*

The noise was so near that we seemed to be standing on top of it. *Where the devil was it coming from?* I played the light over the thorns again, this time more slowly. Something moved on the far side. The beam flicked back and held it: a leafy shoot was jerking to the same erratic rhythm as that strange thumping. I kept the light on it and tried to see through the thorns. They were too dense and a mass of winking pinpoints of reflected light; but the leopard was certainly on the ground at the back of them.

How to get round to it? That the blaze from the torch had not so far worried it was not unusual as leopards will often stand some time staring at a light. But the slightest *sound* would arouse it at once, and to work to the back of the thorns meant leaving the silence of the sandy track for the hazards of leaf and twig-strewn ground.

Somehow we did it—with a luck that seemed miraculous. The light had to be kept on for without it we should never have picked our way. But time and again as we inched round we made small noises which the leopard *must* have heard. Yet it never moved except to keep up that irregular thumping.

The leopard came into the light suddenly. Its head was resting between its outstretched paws and pointing away from us as it lay on the ground. I put the foresight on the back of its neck and then edged nearer until its whole body came into view. My finger tightened on the trigger and then I hesitated. What kind of a leopard was this? During the better part of fifteen minutes, a bright light had been playing about the thorns. Now the light was shining straight at it, and I didn't believe that it had not heard our approach . . . *yet it was still here!*

Some strange fascination held me rooted and kept me staring at its spotted body. The leopard had dragged itself straight through the thorns. Some of the long leafy trailers loaded with claws were wound tightly round one of its hind legs. And now I could see the cause of that thumping. It was the leopard's tail which was hopelessly tangled in a mass of twisted tendrils. It was flicking up and down, but the movements were so listless that it seemed as though the leopard had long since given up hope of wrenching free.

The leopard still had not looked round. It was uncanny, for as we peered round the edge of the thorns we were only twenty paces away. Then almost as if it had read my thoughts, the leopard stirred. With a movement that seemed lazy, it slowly raised its head from between its paws. My finger tightened on the trigger again even though I felt sure that the leopard was still making no move to spring up. Very gently the head shakes from side to side—then turns towards us.

The shock was sudden and complete. I had been ready to see the blazing eyes and snarling mouth of a leopard when it looked into the light. But there were no eyes and no mouth. I caught my breath as the hideous mask turned full towards me. It was a featureless blank of an unearthly dull brown. I stared at it with a wave of horror surging through me. The thing on the ground seemed to be some multiversant devil of the forest in animal guise.

Without realizing that I had squeezed the trigger, I saw the horror in front of me leap to the shock of the bullet. While its legs were still kicking in the air I put in another shot and it lay quiet. Now I had to turn to control the dogs before they raced forward. When I looked again the leopard's breathing had stopped. Slowly I went up to it and, with the muzzle an inch from its neck, trod on the end of its tail. Devil or not there was no longer any life in its body.

I walked up to its head and looked down at the mask. For a few moments I was puzzled until I bent closer. *Poor devil!*

It seemed to have taken nearly every pellet from a birdshot cartridge full in the face. Both eyes had been put out, and it was the second of three animals I have found blinded by criminally careless shooting. I believe, too, that its hearing must have been impaired, although it could not have been stone deaf. It had heard Sammy and had been able to keep near him; and when it had heard that last bark of alarm so near, it had made a desperate attempt to get itself a meal. That the dogs and I had been able to stalk it was not surprising—and nothing we are proud of. The leopard could never have seen us, and the fact that it didn't hear us either was thanks again to the man that fired that wicked shot.

TIGERS' TRAP

It was early one December that the Salichauka Tigress suddenly left her usual haunts. For some time there was no news, though vague rumour reported her heading west. By then she had been a man-eater for over a year, and although her exact toll of human lives was uncertain, she had by now an alarming number of victims to her discredit. An elusive and cunning animal which never returned to a kill, and if trapped in a beat she always broke back or through the stops . . . and heaven help the man within reach who tried to turn her back.

She was certainly heading west, and although none of us here knew it she was moving swiftly towards the estate. As she came, the fierce urge to mate was beginning to stir and honing her temper to a finer edge. Now she was savage and ready to kill simply to vent her feelings and not because she was hungry. In the eight days she took to reach our border, she murdered three more men.

The tiger came from the east. A magnificent specimen in his prime but known to be limping from what was believed to be an old gunshot wound in the right shoulder. His was a quick and uncertain temper too, but although he had every reason to hate humankind, he was not yet preying on man. He was, however, killing cattle in such a bold and wanton way and so intolerant of interference whenever he sailed into a village herd that it seemed but a matter of time before someone got hurt.

The tiger arrived first and announced his coming by killing a cow owned by a small cultivator named Pooram whose land adjoins our northern boundary. When this happened, the tigress was still thirty miles away and had just taken her second victim since leaving her old haunts. Nobody around us was yet very worried for reports about her were still vague; so that night Pooram sat over his dead cow with ‘six fingers of powder’ and a heavy load of assorted shot in his muzzle-loading gun.

Soon after nine o’clock, the tiger strode boldly up to the kill and tried to drag it away. Pooram, hidden low in a tree, switched on his torch. But the moment it went on, the tiger charged with a nerve-shattering roar and sprang at the machan. Pooram was caught completely by surprise and dropped his torch. Then he fired blindly into the darkness at the foot of the tree.

It must have been Pooram’s lucky night. This tiger knew all about ‘lights up trees’ and the men behind them; the wound in his shoulder was a constant and painful reminder and twice since he’d got it, he had sprung at machans. However, the thunderous report and the impressive pyrotechnics of the crude black powder seem to have been beyond his experience; he was scared off and did not come back.

Pooram told me the story the next morning and added that he was pretty sure the tiger ‘hadn’t been hit’. I thought he was probably right: a shot fired blindly into the dark seldom takes effect, but in case he was wrong we searched the jungles over a wide area for most of that day. By six o’clock in the evening we had found no blood and seen no trace of the tiger; we gave the search up and went home.

The tigress, as far as anybody knows, arrived two days later and killed a man at about four in the afternoon. On my way to the scene of the attack, I still knew nothing of her coming and believed the culprit was Pooram's tiger. It must have been hit after all, and now this unfortunate man had blundered into it and paid the price every wounded tiger tries to extort.

But the bloodstained ground told a different story. The only pug marks around were those of a tigress, and where she had made off up a small ravine, the sand showed her carrying the victim in her mouth. By the time I knew that, the sun was below the purple line of the distant hills and so, with less than fifteen minutes of daylight left, it was obviously unwise to follow the drag after a dead man and offer the tigress an easy second chance in the dark. The only course was to return home and make plans for the next morning.

Early that night, however, the affair took a strange turn, and because I'd had no previous experience of a similar situation before, I really did not know what to expect. The tiger and tigress joined up. At nine o'clock I heard her calling from the big nullah and she was answered almost at once by the tiger from the hills beyond. She called twice more, and each time received an eager reply as the tiger moved swiftly towards her. . .

■

What now? Would the next kill be man or beast?

Frankly I didn't know, but it seemed to me that the answer would depend on whether this tigress now behaved as one in love should and pretended that she hadn't got a 'past'. The night before the tiger had undoubtedly taken her under his protection, so to hold her affections it was now his job, and also his pleasure, to show his hunting prowess off before her and incidentally provide all she could want to eat. If she accepted that as she should and did not hunt for herself, then the immediate danger to human life *might* be over until the tigers separated when their love cooled.

On the hopeful assumption that the tiger would now do all the hunting, I had eight buffaloes ready to be tied in the jungle by four o'clock that same afternoon. What happened after that rested in the lap of the forest gods.

In a way they were kind though obviously not prepared to make things too easy. It was again past six o'clock, as I was tying the last buffalo, that three breathless men ran up to say that a tiger had just killed one of their cows in the big nullah. The cow, they added excitedly, had not yet been dragged away because the buffaloes in the herd had driven the tiger off.

Racing back with them, I found the cow not only still there but still alive. For a few moments I could only stare in amazement at the poor beast writhing on the sand. Never before had I seen an animal deliberately savaged by a tiger.

It seemed as though the brute had purposely tried not to kill it. There was no sign of a fang mark, and before the buffaloes had driven him off he had flayed great strips of hide from one side of the cow's body with his claws.

On the surface it was an inexplicably savage assault for the tiger is essentially a clean and tidy killer. To be sure, the mating urge brings on in the male some strange desires to show off. But such a lubberly attack as this would not have impressed the tigress. It certainly didn't impress me: an attack like this, coming as I knew it did from an experienced cattle-killer, was so odd that it immediately suggested something out of the ordinary. As I was trying to think of some explanation, an alarming suspicion leapt into my mind.

A bungling tiger! Everything about the attack pointed to that. The idea was frightening; for if that suspicion was right, then the danger to human life was now far greater than ever before.

That miserable cow was still alive and probably would not die for some time. The owner as usual would not allow me to end its sufferings; it had to be left exactly where and how it was. That meant I should have to watch its struggles, perhaps for many hours, if I sat over it to wait for the tigers. But I wasn't really anxious to wait for them then.

By now, it was almost dark and too late to make any preparations. Besides this, I believed that there was little chance to shoot either of these animals over a tied kill at night. The tigress certainly would never return by herself. Then there was Pooram's experience with the tiger; as that was likely to happen again I might lose them both in the confusion of a sudden charge. It was wiser to wait. The tiger was almost certain to return and drag the cow away. Then, when I'd located it in the morning, I'd try to stalk them on the kill over ground I knew better than they did.

Soon after dawn next morning, I was back on the nullah bank and peeping down from behind a screen of bushes. The sandy bed was empty. Of the cow there was no sign, but from where it had lain the evening before I could see the long marks where the tiger had dragged it away. After I had listened for some time for alarms from the jungle, I worked slowly down the bank and began to study the signs in the sand.

They told a curious story and, but for the suspicion already in my mind, it was one that would normally have misled me entirely and so masked a state of affairs now likely to become an appalling danger. For if that suspicion had not been there I should not have understood what I saw in the sand; for although I have never seen anything like it before, I would have been content to let it pass as some odd streak of cruelty brought out by the fierce urge now coursing through the tiger's blood.

I checked over the story in the sand several times. It was so unusual that I wanted to be sure my deduction was at least somewhere near the truth; but at the end of another twenty minutes I had not been able to alter it. Incredibly the tiger had made a second savaging attack and had failed once more to kill that puny cow. The sand showed his hind legs dancing madly around it, and from the scattered fragments of flesh and skin lying about he had been raining down blow after blow with his forepaws.

No doubt he would have killed it in a few seconds more; but before he could, the tigress strode up, jostled him out of the way, and then sank her fangs in the cow's neck and with a vicious shake despatched it as a tiger should.

There was no doubt that she had done it. Her pug marks were a single clear track above all the other signs around where the cow had lain; and a pool of blood, proof that the victim was still alive when she took over, had dripped from the punctures made by her fangs. The great round pugs of the tiger were clear in the sand some yards away from where he had watched her do the deed. When the cow was dead he never went back to it; the tigress had dragged it away herself while the tiger walked meekly beside her.

That was the story. As I checked it for the last time three questions were clamouring for an answer: Why did a courting tiger allow his mate to do all the things he should have *liked* to do himself? Why had he not once used his teeth? And why could he not kill that miserable cow with a single swipe of a huge paw?

I believed that the answer to the first two questions was *Pooram and his muzzle-loading gun!* By an unlucky fluke he had hit the tiger after all and wounded it about the jaws. The answer to the third question was probably an injury as well: the old wound in his shoulder, at last so crippling that it was difficult to kill with his paws.

If I had read those signs right it was a story loaded with dynamite. This tiger's temper now must be savage indeed and he would be burning to work it off; for apart from the pain of his wounds, he was now unable to show his mate what a fine chap he was or even provide her with food. Here lay the danger. This particular tigress, as soon as she was hungry, was liable to teach him in one easy lesson how very simple it was *to kill a man!*

Turning back to the sands, I saw that the tigress had dragged the cow to the mouth of a small ravine leading off the nullah. Here she had picked it up bodily and, with the tiger a few paces behind, had scrambled up the bank. I followed their tracks to the top and then for fifty yards beyond. The trail led away to the steepest part of a low ridge of hills which follows the winding course of the nullah and rises close beside the right bank.

To set off along the drag was not advisable. From where I stood everything warned against it: the ground, the thick jungle, and above all the probable behaviour of this pair if I was discovered. They would now be on the high ground well above me; so before I stood the slightest chance of success I must know at least roughly where they were and whether one was on the prowl while the other guarded the kill.

I jumped back to the nullah and then set off on a wide detour to bring me to the top of the ridge. What was really going to help now was long familiarity with the ground. This ground, though, is not easy. Most of the thickly wooded ridge rises at nearly forty-five degrees, and about the spot where I thought the tigers might be a prominent hill towers above it. The top of this hill is rounded, and sitting on it like a clown's hat is a gigantic mound. Around the base of this, solid rock rises to some thirty feet and then breaks up into huge boulders with thorny scrub and stunted trees dotted about them. There is only one way to the top: a rocky track trodden out by goats—the only animals which seem to use the mound.

As I made my way along the top of the ridge to the foot of it, I was hoping that I already knew where the tigers were. Below the mound, and about half-way down the hill, is a small natural terrace surrounded by a broken ring of rocks. Inside this the ground is more or less open to the sky, though there are a few shady trees and patches of brush. Outside the rocks the jungle crowds in closely. A natural place to take a kill, and tigers and leopards had used it countless times before.

After I reached the foot of the mound, I scrambled to the top by the spiralling track. There I sat on a boulder and took out the glasses. Below me, the tops of the trees looked like the thick pile of a vast mottled-green carpet ruffled carelessly over the hill. Half-way down was a small oval gap. This was the terrace. But even with the glasses I could not see into it; the slope was too steep and only the upper parts of the trees on the far side were visible.

I kept the glasses trained and started to search about the trees. Almost at once I saw a slight movement in a tree-top to the left of the gap. There was a black dot among the leaves. Then I saw more black dots to the right and left of it. Crows! Many of them waiting patiently for something on the ground. I lowered the glasses and began to listen. Over a wide area around this hill there are always hundreds of jungle chickens and peafowl. These would now be feeding in the undergrowth; and in the trees above them there were sure to be scores of langur monkeys—alarmists all for any danger stalking through the forest. Neither bird nor beast was speaking of any prowling enemy.

I put the glasses away for it was time to start. I now knew where the kill was, and the silence of the jungle and the crows in the trees almost certainly meant that both tigers were lying close beside it.

At the foot of the mound I left the glasses behind a rock and then threw after them everything from my pockets that might rattle or clink. From where I was on the shoulder of the hill, the best ground for a stalk to the terrace below curled round in a wide arc and gave me some 500 yards to go. It was just nine o'clock, and as I started out I was hoping that by now both those tigers would be asleep after a heavy meal.

All the details of how I went are not important. It is enough to say that the stalk took over two hours and that I did not take a single chance in case the tigers were not as close to the kill as I thought. If they had been higher up the hill and not together it would have been all too easy, over that broken ground, to blunder past them. That might have ended the game: a sudden rush by both of them, perhaps from different directions, would have been difficult to stop in time.

At last it was over when, from behind the cover of some thorns, one end of the terrace came into view about seventy yards below me. At the same moment I saw the tiger. He was lying under the shade of a small tree, flicking his tail to keep off the flies. The rest of the terrace was screened by a heap of rocks dotted with small bushes right in front of me. As I was badly placed to go forward, I eased back and crept round behind the thorns; then I crawled towards the rocks from the other side and slowly pulled myself to the top of them.

The tigress was there. She was stretched on a patch of grass beside the kill, her white belly a brilliant mark against the vivid green. For a few seconds, I stared down at both animals weighing the chances. I could kill the tigress with the first shot, but would there be time after that to reload and get on the tiger before he was into the trees?

All at once it came to me that to bolt might be the last thing this tiger would do. With a fresh wound and the fire of the mating urge still burning strongly, he would be out for revenge the second he saw that the tigress was either dead or injured. The 'double' must depend on whether the shot brought the tiger bounding up the hill; if it did there were seventy yards in which to stop him.

Then a drongo bird told the tigers where I was.

I had just started to slide the rifle over the top of the rocks when the creeping barrel scared it. With a shrill screech and flapping wings it sailed up from a bush a little beyond and below my cover. In the twinkling of an eye, its urgent alarm had warned every living thing around of the intruder behind the rocks.

Both tigers were on their feet in a flash. For a fleeting second, they stared up towards my cover. Although only the top of my hat was showing above the rocks, it seemed that they picked me out at once. Then they were gone—one to the right and the other to the left.

It was all so sudden that for a few precious seconds I just stared down at the empty terrace. Then came the realization that the next moment might see the tigers racing in from right and left. I sprang up and started to run. After a few yards I flung my hat to the rocks: the tigers would find it and check for a few vital seconds to sniff at the hated human taint. After that I was climbing as never before towards the mound —obeying the instincts of a hunted animal by racing for the highest ground. It was in any case the best course for I had no idea what the tigers were actually doing. It was not impossible that they were running away from me; and it might also be true that they didn't yet know me for a man and imagined that something had been after their kill. Even so, a sudden meeting—whether the nature of their quarry surprised them or not—would not for a second keep either of them off.

I reached the foot of the mound dripping with sweat and with my lungs ready to burst. I slowed for breath: only a little farther and the advantage would be back in my hands once I was on the mound. If the tigers really were out for trouble they would have to use the track to reach me.

As I ran on towards the foot of the track a sudden sneezing chatter broke out to my left. *Monkeys!* Their alarm for one of the big cats. Almost immediately after it came a loud clucking from the right as a frightened jungle hen fled before something moving swiftly behind it.

I leaped for the track and tore round the first loop until I came to a spot thirty feet up and covering the start of it below. Here I got down beside a rock and pushed the rifle forward.

From this position I could see not only the foot of the track but wide sweeps of the jungle on the shoulders of the hill to my right and left.

Kok-Kok-Kok-Kok-Kaaaaak! The frightened screech of a peacock from the jungle just below. Then I heard its mad scamper through the undergrowth change to the frantic beating of wings and a second later it sailed out of the trees and passed overhead. The tigress came into view a second after weaving fast across the slope of the hill. She was almost up to the foot of the track when she checked. She had seen me, the drop of my head after looking at the peacock. Before I could get her in my sights, she was behind cover. Then I saw her again moments after flitting through the trees to the right. I had to let her go; between us was a tangle of trunks and leaves.

When she was out of sight I heard her call from the back of the mound. But the sound was like nothing I had ever heard from a tigress before: a drawn-out mewing cough which vibrated with a strangely sinister note. At the time I had no idea what it meant. Now I think I know what she was doing—telling the tiger where I was.

Even today I am still not sure what was in the minds of those tigers or even whether they were in fact after my blood. One thing, however, I do know, and that is if the attack which came soon after was deliberately aimed at me, then it was the most frightening exhibition I ever want to see of two tigers hunting as a pair in perfect co-ordination and understanding. At the time it certainly seemed that they were hunting me, and it seemed, too, that I was in their trap only a few minutes after the tigress passed out of sight.

When the jaws of the trap were about to snap shut, I was lying across the track with my eyes on the start of it thirty feet below. Suddenly the tigress called again. This time the sound brought me bounding to my feet to stare upwards in utter disbelief. The tigress was not only on the mound but on the next loop of the track above my head!

How she got there I did not understand. Nevertheless, she was now above me and I caught a fleeting glimpse of her as she looked over the edge of the track above me. Then she dodged back. But the surprise had been complete, and there was to be little time to recover.

The sudden squeaking alarm of some babbler birds snapped my eyes to the right. *Something was coming along the track!* I could see twenty yards before it bent round a corner of rock. An instant later the tiger came round in a swift creeping crouch. There was just the slightest check when he saw me. Then he was coming on. At ten yards, in that most dangerous moment of all when eye meets eye, he threw up his head and shattered the air with a bellowed *AOUFF!*

I fired as the toss of his head uncovered his chest. The bullet caught him with his muscles bunched and sprang him high in the air. At the top of his leap his outstretched fore legs dropped like a wounded bird's and the roar trailed to a choking grunt. He thumped down like a heavy sack half over the edge of the track where he hung fighting feebly for a hold. Then he was gone, tumbling down the sheer rock face to the start of the track thirty feet below.

As the crash of the report was still echoing round the hills, I saw the tigress again from the corner of my eye. She was just where I had seen her last for the shot had brought her forward to peer down. Only her head was visible, and even as the bolt clattered and the spent case tinkled to the rocks she was drawing back. An awkward straight-up swing at a small target disappearing fast. The bullet burst a rock into a puff of dust and flying splinters where her head had been a fraction before.

Then there were only the rocks and bushes above and the sun shining into my eyes. I waited with my back pressed hard against the rock. An ominous silence was all round. The minutes ticked away to five, but there was still no sign of the tigress. All at once I saw her again. But now she was off the mound and down on the left shoulder of the hill loping away fast through the trees. She would not come back; after that last shot the cunning of the man-eater was driving her away from a danger she knew only too well.

But even as she went she was going to her death. On the way back to her old haunts, she was trapped in a casual beat. No one knew she was there. She tried her old tricks but was wounded; then she turned and mauled the sportsman who had shot her before she died.

When I reached the foot of the track, I examined the tiger. He was a fine animal, with massive shoulders and forelegs as thick as any I have seen; but fine as he was, I had undoubtedly shot the wrong one. Later, however, when I looked him over more closely, I wondered if I had been so wrong after all. He had been hit by nine of Pooram's very assorted pellets. Some were about the nose, but three of the largest had lodged close together in the left joint of the jaw. With his skin off, the older wound in his shoulder was a spongy yellow mass with a 12-bore 'lethal' ball deeply embedded in splintered bone. Cattle now would have been beyond him. To keep alive he would have had to seek some easier and lighter prey; with the tigress around to help him there would undoubtedly have been a great deal of trouble. Before I left the mound, I set off to find how the tigers had got up. I was still puzzled, for I had always believed that no big cat could scale the sheer rock faces. But they didn't have to: towards the back there was a wide cleft six feet up with an overhang of dense lantana and thorns screening it completely. I had never noticed it before, but with unerring animal instinct the tigers had spotted it. Perhaps one, or even both, had used it before. Some carnivora certainly had. Beyond the cleft was a natural place to take a kill, as old bones about the ground showed. Inside it was dark and dank, the air fetid. The place suddenly depressed me: this would have been the spot to drag anything killed on the mound.

MONKEY'S FOLLY

Soon after coming to Mandikhera, Babs and I spent several days exploring it with the map. From the start this map had intrigued us. It had come with the title deeds and looked like an old chart to some pirate's treasure. It was drawn in faded ink on yellowing parchment and was covered with figures and odd hieroglyphics; there were also mysterious references like Old Diggings and Not Here. At two places there were crosses, and at another the remark 'no good'.

For us, however, this map had one serious defect. There was not, apart from the Denwa River, a single spot on the estate with a name. We decided to put that right; for how otherwise should we be able to explain where anything had happened unless the whole place was properly labelled with Devil's Punchbowls and Lover's Leaps?

To start with, it looked as though our task was going to be easy. After one glance at the mound on the ridge, we licked our pencil and marked it in as 'Spy-Glass Hill'. Then we were stuck, for it is not at all easy to name bare scenery on the spur of the moment with something that fits. At the end of three days, we were not much farther forward and the map had only a few obvious names on it like The Pool, The Big Nullah, Rocky Ford, and the Old Well.

For the next month or so, more important things claimed our attention and the map was put away. Then, without any help from us, places started to name themselves. Creaking Tree Hill was the first. This is a small stony promontory on the ridge with a dozen or so trees on it. One of these creaks loudly, and on a still day can be heard for over a quarter of a mile. What actually creaks we still don't know; the sound comes up through the rocks from underground and is probably made by two roots rubbing together as the tree sways in the wind.

Next came Sambur Deep. This is a densely wooded patch with thick undergrowth that lies in an elbow formed by the big nullah. This place almost always holds sambur which are the largest and shyest deer we have. Not far from here is Dhobi's Leap. This got its name from a washerman who once worked for us, a likeable old reprobate called Biro. Most of the time he was under the influence of 'jungle juice' and was reputedly his own best customer at a secret still he ran as a sideline in the depths of the forest. One day he limped home with his clothes torn and covered with blood. He had been strolling through the forest, he said, when a sambur sprang up and started to chase him. He had only got away by leaping down a sheer rock face into the branches of a tree below. Nobody is yet sure whether the sambur was a real one or not.

Whistling Wood, as the name suggests, is another spot you can hear and went down on the map early. This wood is a small one of about two acres with a giant pipul tree towering up from the centre. One night during a violent storm this tree was struck by lightning and set on fire. It was not, however, completely destroyed; a lashing rain soon quenched the flames and so saturated the ground below it that the gale nearly blew it over; it stands today leaning at some forty-five degrees. A part of the tree died and left one blackened limb pointing at the sky. In a short time termites hollowed this out and left it with a peculiar characteristic.

When the wind from a certain direction has built up to a proper strength, a few melodious notes suddenly boom out. If you've got some imagination the sound is not unlike the opening bars of 'Ave Maria' played on an organ. After dark, even though you know what it is, the sound becomes eerie and vaguely disturbing; in a storm it is positively frightening, for then it builds up into a high whistling shriek which conjures up all the demons in hell.

To the north side of Whistling Wood is Piccadilly Circus. Here, five game tracks meet, and if you want to watch animals at night, this is the place to sit. However, a stranger should always leave his imagination at home for there are few spells when something is not on the move near by and you don't always see it or know what it is. This keeps you on edge and tends to make you forget the whistling tree which booms suddenly and without warning. A stranger must beware of something else, too. Before he sits he will almost certainly have heard from one of the forest folk about the little white grave near the pipul. In this rest the ashes of a great hunter whose last wish was to remain among the jungles and the animals he had loved so well. Local superstition now says that a shadowy figure stalks through the darkness under the trees with a rifle at the ready.

Monkey's Folly is another place that named itself. This lies right at the end of the big nullah where it runs out into the river. Around here there is always a troop of monkeys. From the high branches of the koha trees lining the banks, they can see a long stretch of the riverbed and any danger coming along it; to monkeys that means tigers and leopards creeping up to start the long stalk up the nullah. A lot of alarms begin here and are taken up from troop to troop for more than three miles.

That brings us to the Yellow Basket. He was a leopard in the same class as the badmash, every bit as cunning and perhaps a trifle bolder. Now all leopards are bad, but some stick in your mind more than others for some piece of villainy right out of the ordinary run. We christened the Yellow Basket rather too early, for he got this name when he was being just an ordinary nuisance; towards the end, however, he had done something so terrible that we dropped the euphemism and called him what we really meant.

This leopard had been about for some time and, to start with, had been content with an occasional goat. Then he committed his first act of real villainy. We had just bought our first pedigree cow and the Basket took her on the third day. To us it seemed like deliberate selection, for the cow was mixed up in a herd of some fifty 'nothing special' animals.

The kill took place after the herd had left the cowsheds and within two hundred yards of the house. It had been both clumsy and noisy for the Basket was the small type of 'village' leopard and really had no business to be trying for cattle. He dragged it only twenty-five yards; then the cowherds, who were not quite sure what had happened, rushed up and drove him off. Even so, in the short time that elapsed for them to race to the house and me to rush back with a rifle, the Basket had returned and begun to feed.

It looked an easy one. There was a suitable tree near by, and within fifteen minutes my machan chair had been hoisted up and I was waiting for the leopard to come back and finish his meal. Several times he was not far away: once, two frightened peafowl ran from cover and dashed past the kill, and on half a dozen occasions monkeys near by spoke of their worst enemy. But first the lunch hour and then teatime went by with still no sight of him. Then the sun started to sink below the trees.

Not much later the whole jungle was filled with the ruddy glow from a glorious sunset. Soon it was gone and then the grey of dusk was deepening into night. All at once I noticed something odd: a patch of sunlight had been left behind on the toe of my right boot. I stared at it in surprise, not understanding; then I wiggled my foot and the sunlight disappeared.

I looked down at the rifle lying beside me on the small platform that supported my chair. It was resting on the switch of the torch and the light was on. When I picked up the rifle the batteries were nearly exhausted; the bulb showed only a dull red glow. This time I had no spare torch although I never sit up without one. But who would think such a thing necessary when starting a sit-up at ten o'clock in the morning? Indeed, the torch on the rifle was only there at all because it goes on every night in case of a sudden alarm; now, just when I should probably need it, it was useless.

The Basket came when it was really dark. The time was a few minutes after eight; for I had decided that if he had not come by nine, I should give him up and go home. The kill now was quite invisible as it lay under a patch of shadow and not even the light from the stars touched it. I did not hear him coming, but the sudden sound of tearing flesh told me that he had arrived.

What was left of the moon would not rise until after midnight. By then the Basket would almost certainly have finished his meal and be gone. For as long as I could, I resisted the temptation to fire blind at the sounds of feeding; the chance would be far better if he showed himself under the stars even for a few seconds. But after listening to him for half an hour, I could stand it no longer; it seemed impossible to miss an animal the size of a leopard from less than twenty yards, even in the dark.

I did not hurry the shot. I knew, after having looked at it all day, exactly where the kill lay. Towards this spot I pointed the muzzle of the rifle and then, by turning first one ear and then the other, aimed at the sounds of feeding. Then, holding steady and with the greatest care, I squeezed the trigger.

As I have said before, this kind of shooting seldom scores and it didn't now. I heard the leopard spring away obviously unharmed. That he'd had a nasty fright I did not doubt: the crashing report must have burst in his face and there had been a blinding flash from the muzzle; then had come the clatter of the bolt and the tinkle of the empty case as it fell to the ground through the branches.

But a really bold leopard is unpredictable. After a little more than fifteen minutes, I heard him come back. I could scarcely believe my ears; for although I have known leopards come back after being fired at, I had never had one return so soon. That stung me enough to try another shot—and I missed again. This time the leopard sprang away with a deep growl—but almost at once he was back and carrying on with his meal as though nothing had happened.

There was now only one cartridge left in the magazine and I resisted the temptation to use it. But for all the good that came of keeping it, I might just as well have fired it off. The Basket never showed himself once and went on eating until I thought he would burst. As a final insult, he cleaned his claws on a tree not far from mine and then strolled away with a loud belch.

For several months after that, the Basket kept fairly quiet although he was still hanging about. In the normal course of events, I should have kept after him for his presence was a constant danger to the stock; but at this time I was still doing nightwatchman round the fields.

It was late one evening that the awful thing happened. The Basket took Bimbo. Not Bimbo the langur monkey, but a little cairn terrier of the same name. What was so bad about this was that Bimbo did not belong to us but to some old friends, Nancy and Tirrel Hawkins who had been staying with us.

Nancy and Tirrel stayed several weeks and then had to return to Jubbulpore; but as their plans were unsettled, they asked us to look after Bimbo. We gladly agreed to have him, he was a grand little dog and by now had become one of the family. However . . . Bimbo had one very bad habit: he loved to bark at monkeys—which is about the quickest way of all to call up a leopard.

Now, all our own dogs bark at monkeys too if they think they can get away with it. Indeed, this habit is not an easy one to break completely because monkeys deliberately tease and seem to have some strange power that tempts a dog to be disobedient. Our dogs, however, are well aware of the 'monkey-stick' behind the door and of the high price that even a small bark costs. Of this stick Bimbo knew nothing, and as a 'guest' we hardly liked to tell him; so to play it safe we decided to take no risks and keep him either in a small compound near the house or tied up beside us on the veranda.

It was a day several weeks later that Shirley and Ada Granville from Pachmarhi dropped in for lunch and tea. For most of that day we just sat on the veranda and talked. Bimbo was tied up at one end of it and as usual he was very good; that was how we came to forget him until after tea. Then Babs remembered that he had not been out since before lunch.

When he was let off the lead, he stayed for some time near my chair waiting for me to take him for his usual evening walk. That evening, however, I did not go out but stayed talking to Shirley and Ada until they left at about seven o'clock. No one saw Bimbo leave, but he must eventually have got fed up with waiting and then wandered off on his own. At first we were not worried. Bimbo had been away on his own before, and although the danger from leopards is ever present, these pests are fortunately not so numerous as to be everywhere all the time. Besides, when we looked round, our dogs were missing, too; that surely meant they were all together and there was safety in numbers.

At seven-forty-five, our dogs came tearing back to the house. Something obviously was wrong: all of them were very excited and Jill was whimpering. There was no sign of Bimbo, though by now it was nearly dark. All at once we were worried. Very worried indeed; and at eight o'clock, when Bimbo had still not come home, we called all the men up to the house and then set off to search with lanterns and torches.

By midnight, we still had found no sign of him though we had by now called through every likely spot. As we turned for home there was no doubt in any of our minds that Bimbo had been taken. Babs and I were very upset. To lose a dog of your own is a heart-breaking experience; to lose one belonging to someone else makes it a thousand times worse.

Soon after dawn the next morning I was out again. I still had no clue to where Bimbo had been taken from, and it was after midday before I found the first signs of the leopard. He had drunk at a small pool right at the end of the big nullah where it joins the river; it was another hour before I was sure that Bimbo was dead.

For several reasons I decided not to sit up. Instead, I tied a goat at a spot near by to which I could creep up from behind cover. During the afternoon I visited this spot several times and always found the goat alive. After tea I stayed near it, but out of sight, listening for some sign that would tell of the leopard's coming. But he did not come, nor had there been a single alarm from anywhere around when I went home after dark. As far as I could tell the leopard did not return during the night although by dawn the next morning my goat was dead; it had been killed by a pair of hyenas.

I did not tie out another. The weather was still cold and I thought I stood a better chance to get the leopard when he was taking the morning sun somewhere along the top of the ridge. So, each day at dawn when I came off the fields, I stalked along it with the rising sun at my back and the prevailing westerly wind blowing into my face; under foot the ground and the dead leaves would be soaked with a heavy dew. Ideal conditions for stalking, and I was quite sure that soon or late something was going to tell me when the leopard was about.

More than a week went by with no sign of him, so I started to haunt the ridge in the evenings as well. My luck was no better; it began to look as though the leopard had moved away to a healthier spot. The break eventually came one freezing cold morning soon after dawn.

Nothing had actually warned me that the leopard was about and I discovered him quite by chance. At one place the ridge is very narrow and falls steeply away from the path on each side. As I was crossing this, I noticed a ber bush laden with its small plum-like fruits half-way down the slope to my left. The plump red berries looked so nice that I decided to pick some for our two parrots. Before starting the climb down I had a good look all round—and it was then that I spotted the leopard.

He was almost hidden in a small ravine about half-way down the slope. I thought at first that he was asleep for he was quite still and it was difficult to see him; the ravine was overgrown with lantana and only a small part of him was showing. But he was not asleep. A few moments later he started to creep forward and I soon saw why: he was beginning to stalk towards some monkeys on a kossum tree at the foot of the ridge.

It was not possible from where I was to be sure of a shot; for although the ravine was shallow, it was so overgrown that the creeping leopard was more often than not behind cover. But I knew what he was after, and just a little way ahead a sunken path near the bottom of another ravine leads down from the ridge and would bring me out near the tree the monkeys were on.

I was almost there when the monkeys screamed their alarm. The leopard had been discovered. I hurried down the path as fast as I dared, hoping that he had not claimed a victim, for if he had I was going to be too late for he would already be away.

When I got towards the end of the sunken path, the monkeys were still screaming. Now I could see the tree and it was alive with flashing grey figures tearing about it in panic; a few of the wiser monkeys were staying high up, but chattering with rage and shaking the branches furiously. I watched these and saw that they were all looking towards a spread of bushes some fifty yards away to my right. Although I could not see him, I knew that the leopard was somewhere there and that he had not yet caught a monkey.

Now, unless you have actually seen it happen, it is perhaps difficult to believe that a leopard can catch a monkey on a tree. Nevertheless, monkeys do get caught frequently; for the leopard is their most deadly enemy and the mere sight of him strikes so much terror into their hearts that they often act like lunatics. Sometimes one of them may actually fall off the tree with fright; but more often than not the leopard's success comes from a piece of fatheaded reasoning which time and again tempts monkeys to their death.

They are, of course, perfectly safe if they stay where they are, high in the branches. But not all of them do stay. There is often the odd one which, crazy with fear, casts desperately around for some way of escape. Suddenly he thinks he sees it and says to himself: *That tree over there is safer than this one. . .*

I saw the fool start from the top branches and work his way down the tree. When he reached one of the lowest limbs he went out slowly along it, as far from the leopard as he could get. Then, with a quick glance over his shoulder, he leapt to the ground and started to run.

The leopard was out from cover like a streak of lightning. He had the monkey before it had gone twenty yards. For a moment, he checked in his stride to shake it. In that moment, Bimbo's slayer died with the monkey still clamped in his teeth. Later that day I got out the map and marked in the name of Monkey's Folly.

THE THREE BEARS

If there is anything engraved on my heart when I die, it will probably be the word 'peanuts'. Certainly I shall never forget that first crop which kept me on the fields at night, with only a rare break, for nearly six months. For the nightwatchmen never really returned to work except for an occasional few days at a time; after the boar was dead there were several other scares, and it was always some time before the cause of them either went away or was shot. That year of course we were still very inexperienced, and it had been the height of folly to plant peanuts in fields so widely scattered about the jungle. But we certainly had our share of bad luck, too; for soon after the boar came a tigress with two cubs which hung about for more than four months. Actually she gave no trouble and was quite content to mind her own business and her cubs. I know that was true because she must have seen and heard me moving about the jungles on countless occasions. Yet she never so much as warned me off; but as a tigress with cubs is always potentially dangerous, the nightwatchmen still had a legitimate excuse to keep away from their work.

Eventually this tigress was shot. To say that I was sorry she was dead may sound strange. Yet sorry I was: in four long months of wandering through the jungles at night I had not once been threatened by her, and when at last I met her in the dark she would have given way and taken her cubs with her. But the encounter came suddenly and I was excited and unsure what she was going to do; for a very silly reason I pulled the trigger without meaning to. The tigress died, but it was like shooting down a sporting opponent without the chance that she had given me time after time.

When this happened, the rains were over and the cold weather had started. With it came more trouble—even though the tigress was dead. That year the rains had been good, and it was also the coldest year we have had so far. Both these facts now combined to make the nightly rounds of the fields more uncomfortable and hazardous. All at once the nights were freezing, and after the muggy heat of the monsoon I was soon going about with a permanent cold. I didn't really mind the cold for itself, but streaming eyes affected my sight and my hearing suffered, too. The heavy rains had made the jungle almost impassable. The paths I was using were mainly game-tracks, and as the rain poured down these had become steadily more overgrown; when the cold weather set in, long sections of them were actually tunnels through the undergrowth. Eventually I had these cleared, but the way across Witch's Waste seemed to keep pace with the axe and finally beat me.

Witch's Waste is an area of nearly a hundred acres. The previous year it had been heavy forest, but several months before the rains we had cut the trees as the first step to putting it under cultivation. Inexperience again; for after cutting the trees we gave the land a light ploughing before removing the stumps. After the very first shower the brown earth seemed to explode into a thick carpet of weeds. I had never seen anything grow so fast; almost overnight the whole place became a hopeless tangle of what were undoubtedly the most vigorous weeds in the world; and in the end nearly every one produced something that made it difficult to walk through them. Some had thorns, either long or short, curved or straight; others had small and easily detached pods covered with short stiff spikes; another variety of this had big pods with long spikes. One giant plant produced a thing that looked exactly like a snake's skull with two needle-sharp fangs. The list could go on, but it's enough to say that nearly everything clung to or tore clothing, and could either prick, rip, or sting.

At this time, Witch's Waste had not been named. To start with we could think of nothing really suitable to describe a tangled waste it was difficult to walk through. Indeed, as the place grew steadily worse and more impenetrable, it seemed to us that the old-time topographers had the best answer: whenever they came up against a tough bit of country which they were not too keen to explore, they simply marked it down as 'Here Be Dragons' and left it at that. We were often tempted to follow this example, but before we could succumb this place named itself as so many others had done before it.

It was during the scare with the Salichauka Tigress. At the time rumour said that she was near when in fact she was still far away. That, however, did not prevent a report coming in early one morning that she had crossed the river and gone into cover right at the end of this tangled waste. I wanted to beat her out, but when all the men were assembled, Mitu frightened them by saying that the place was haunted by some of the worst demons in the forest. Although I suspected that something was wrong I could not change their minds: whenever jungle men confront you with demons you might just as well chuck your hand in at once and save time. In the end I went after the tigress alone: but when I came to the spot where she was supposed to have gone into the undergrowth, I decided at once that it would be very unwise to go after her.

However, just for the look of things I went in a little way—and got one of the biggest frights I've ever had. For I had not gone far when there was a sudden stealthy movement under a clump of lantana bushes only a few yards away. A second later, I caught sight of something yellow inside them. I fired at once, praying that the shot would pin the tigress down. I heard the bullet strike with a loud *crack!* A moment later there came a vicious hiss and then from the bushes there burst a huge cloud of smoke and steam. I stood rooted to the spot, convinced at last of the supernatural and quite sure that I had stumbled across a witch's cauldron.

Well, it was a sort of cauldron. One of four side by side over a long fire: big yellow earthenware pots in which a real witch's brew was bubbling: a crude jungle distillery, its frightened crew huddled under the bushes near by with sheepish grins on their faces. Mitu's brother was among them, and there is little doubt that Mitu himself and all the other men who refused to beat must have known what was going on. Luckily no one was hurt. It must, however, have been a near thing: my bullet had shattered the first pot, and spilling its contents over the fire had produced that loud hiss and the smoke and steam. After that Witch's Waste seemed a good name, though Here Be Dragons would not have been such a bad choice after all. . .

By the time the cold weather came and the rains had done their worst with Witch's Waste, I liked the one tangled path through it less each time I used it; and I had to use it three times a night as it was part of my regular route and led to a field of peanuts, some eight acres in extent, right at the end of the estate. This path was a dog's leg and formed two sides of a triangle with the field at its apex. Thorn bushes choked it nearly every foot of the way and going along it was both difficult and painful. A great many of these thorns were ber, and after the abundant rains they were loaded with fruit.

It was these ber bushes that eventually brought the last lot of trouble. Deer and antelope love the fruit and will go a long way to get it. Hyenas and jackals eat it too, but the biggest gluttons of all are bears which camp right among the bushes and stay until the fruit is finished. While there is any left, tigers and leopards are never far away. These, of course, are not after the fruit, but as the deer and antelope move from one feeding ground to another, the big cats move with them.

As the ber fruit ripened, so the animals started coming to Witch's Waste in increasing numbers. By this time I had been doing nightwatchman for over four months and my nerves were getting badly frayed. I was also short of sleep: for although I went to bed soon after breakfast each morning, there was always something to be done at home or about the farm; what with one reason or another I seldom got my head down for more than three or four hours a day.

Night by night, as I went through Witch's Waste, I heard more and more animals moving about near me. Most of these I knew were harmless ones like deer and antelope; but unless I actually saw them I was never sure what they were. This uncertainty made the journey very unpleasant, for the great fear that haunted my mind was the possibility of running into a bear.

Now it may seem that a bear would never allow a man to run into it. All wrong. A bear at night is very quarrelsome when feeding and it usually eats in company with other bears. Among themselves they make a great deal of noise; they are very greedy and fight continually to keep the best places to themselves. As they have few natural enemies, they pay little attention to what is going on outside their immediate circle. Add to that a poor eyesight and not particularly good ears and it becomes only too easy to get very close to a bear indeed as there are periods when they are just eating and not making much noise. What happens after that is usually a matter of luck. The bear may not catch you, but if it does and you get away alive, few of your friends will recognize you after. . .

What could I use to tell the bears that no friend was approaching? The bare noise of approach by itself was not enough: other things, of which the bears were not afraid, were moving about, too. At last I had an idea: none of these other things could speak, and if there's one sound that really terrifies wild animals, that sound is the human voice. That is what I decided to use. But I was not proposing to walk round talking to myself; there was, fortunately, a better way than that. . .

At the beginning of the year we had found two baby parrots which had fallen out of their nest. They were very young indeed and quite the ugliest birds we had ever seen. Their heads were shiny and bald, their necks scraggy and wrinkled, their eyes protruded; and a monstrous red-tipped beak bulged from their faces like a tippler's nose. They resembled nothing so much as two of the oldest members straight from the window of some exclusive London club. After scarcely a moment's thought, we christened them Plunkett and Plumleigh.

Of the two, Plumleigh developed quicker and was by far the more intelligent. Indeed, by the time he was a few months old he had become a very useful bird and I often took him with me when sitting up; with Plumleigh around sleep was impossible if he thought there was a melon seed in one of my pockets. He would search every one of them thoroughly, and when he didn't find it he would hop back to my shoulder and bite my ear. If I was still feeling sleepy after that, all I had to do was to show him the seed again.

When the parrots were still very young, they were secured with tiny chains to a perch on the veranda. From there they could hear the wild parrots screaming overhead and gossiping in the orchards. At first they took no notice, but as they grew older they started to answer back and became rather restless. We wondered how they would behave if they were free and whether they would return home at night like the two peacocks and the blue-rock pigeons on the roof. The only way to find out was to let them go and see what happened. But we didn't want to lose them, so the night before the experiment we dyed them red. Outside there are hundreds of green parrots, and if ours decided to stay out too long we wanted to be sure that we were chasing the right ones.

Plumleigh, while he was being dipped, protested violently. We didn't really blame him: it's not easy to dye a green parrot red, and several dips were necessary before we were satisfied. When at last we were, he was speechless with rage, but once back on his perch he started to splutter. To us it sounded suspiciously like: *By Gad, sir—what a damned impertinence!*

Plunkett, on the other hand, gave no trouble at all and seemed anxious to co-operate. We were not really surprised: some time before a friend who is a keen bird-watcher had told us that 'he' was a 'she'. Now there was little doubt that he was right; for once Plunkett was back beside Plumleigh, she preened her feathers carefully and obviously liked her new coat; as she titivated up her expression was distinctly smug and it was quite plain that she was planning how best to pin back the ears of 'that Mrs. Jones next door'.

The next day, Plumleigh refused to go out. He just sat sulking on his perch, glaring at us with furious eyes. Plunkett never hesitated, and in three not-too-confident flights made the bottom orchard. Here she sat for more than an hour in a guava tree. She was showing off her red coat to several parrots which came to have a look at her. Then, all of a sudden, she fluttered down and obviously wanted to be taken home. She was not actually in tears, but we rather thought she must have overheard some remark like: 'My dear!—how *does* she do it on what *he* makes?'

Perhaps, though, she had been frightened by the crows. They were even more interested than the parrots and would very likely have killed her. After that we kept the pair of them on the veranda. Plunkett remained very proud of her new coat; but it was more than a week before Plumleigh forgave us for his; in fact, each time I spoke to him while the outrage still rankled, he answered me back with a curt *sonofabitch!*

Although Plumleigh was obviously being rude, I was always pleased to hear him trot this out because I had taken some trouble to teach him how to say it. Which brings me back, after a rather long digression, to the human voice and the bears in Witch's Waste. Plumleigh was the answer. If I took him with me there would be no need to walk round talking to myself, and it would be a good opportunity to go on with his lessons which of late had been badly neglected. Indeed, most of his party-piece, which had been chosen for him after some careful thought, was still to be mastered. It was that neat little rhyme that goes:

If you want to get rich, you son of a bitch,
I'll tell you what to do:
Never sit down with a tear or a frown,
And paddle your own canoe.

Plumleigh never had the slightest difficulty with the s.o.b. part and would have been quite content to let the whole matter end with that. But I wanted him word perfect, and now that we were going to have the time, there was no reason why he should not learn it all and then go on to something more ambitious that would really astonish his friends.

It was surprising what a difference having him with me made. He was the very thing I had always wanted, something that was flesh and blood and which could answer back when spoken to. Nor was he ever the slightest trouble for he seemed to enjoy coming round with me at night; he liked to travel either on my shoulder snuggled against my neck or up on my hat if the weather was not too cold. Not once did he try to fly away, and he never showed any signs of fear even when something was moving near us or when some startling sound ripped out of the jungle.

However, I was not sure how he would react to a shot fired near him. So before I went up to any field where there might be some business with the pigs, I always left Plumleigh well behind me on some perch high off the ground. I still think it was a wise precaution: a shot fired with him on my shoulder must have sent him flying off into the night perhaps never to be found again; but it was this precaution that nearly led me into the arms of a bear.

It was early one morning shortly before dawn and the moon had set about an hour previously. It was dark though not black, and Plumleigh and I were making our last journey through Witch's Waste. Once we had investigated the field at the top of it we should be on the last lap and heading towards home and breakfast. As usual I switched off the torch some hundred and fifty yards from the field and stopped to listen.

A fresh morning breeze was blowing full in our faces and for a few moments I heard nothing except Plumleigh rambling on about some rich sonofabitch paddling a canoe. He was horribly mixed. But there was no time to correct him now: the breeze had suddenly brought the distinct sounds of pig hard at work on my peanuts. I shut Plumleigh up and started to move on, looking as I went to the right and left of the path for some suitable place to leave him. Thirty yards down the path on the left side a high bush suddenly loomed up above the thick undergrowth. It was some twenty paces from the path and I had to push my way through the undergrowth to reach it.

It was a thorn bush. Plumleigh, however, never minded thorns so I felt about for a perch. My left hand soon found one and I hoisted him up to it balanced on my right forefinger. When he was comfortably settled I whispered *There you are, Plummy*, and turned back to the path.

The second after I spoke the bush seemed to explode. Only those who have actually heard a bear scream into hysterics can know what the noise is like. It's an appalling medley of screams, grunts, growls and barks, that can haunt your dreams for nights after. The bear had been on the other side of the bush—less than two yards away. Fortunately it made off at once and my torch was just in time to pick up its stern before it disappeared into the undergrowth.

It was a nasty scare, and I don't mind admitting that it left me shaking. I have seen the faces and scalps of several jungle men who have been mauled by bears which they have come upon unawares. All of them had been maimed and badly disfigured, living warnings of what a bear can do when it comes to grips.

When I was eating breakfast, I seriously considered leaving those eight acres at the end of Witch's Waste to their fate. To keep on alone, even with Plumleigh's help, was plainly asking for trouble. But I don't like to be beaten; so, by the time I was getting ready for bed, I was wondering whether any of the men could be persuaded to come round with me. Bhutu, I knew, would jump at the chance; but to take him off his day work would disorganize several jobs we then had on hand. Before going to sleep, I asked Babs to sound Tulsi. He was a stolid young chap who had been with us from the start and who might agree to come; he was dead keen on any kind of shikar and had plenty of guts.

When I woke up for tea, Babs told me that Tulsi was coming round with me. I was pleased to hear that, and as soon as tea was over I called him up and told him what I wanted him to do. I must, however, confess that I did not tell him that I was now too scared to go through Witch's Waste alone; instead, I told him that I needed two additional weapons and wanted him to carry the shotgun and the .22 rifle. This at least was half the truth. These weapons really were needed: to deal with a sounder of pig at close quarters there is nothing like a shotgun, but beyond thirty yards it is ineffective and only a rifle will do. The .22 was for jackals and porcupines. These animals damage peanuts, too, but at this time both 12-bore and rifle cartridges were difficult to get and I had not been using them against anything but pig. Now, with the .22 loaded with hollow-point bullets, I should be able to deal with these smaller pests as well.

For exactly eleven days, this new arrangement worked well. With an instant choice of weapons I was having more success than I had ever had before. And what a difference a real live man behind me made! For the first time I was almost enjoying the night rounds.

Then, on the night of the eleventh day, we ran into trouble.

The time was about midnight. In the sky above us was a waxing moon which cast a silvery radiance over the jungle, but out of its light the shadows were hard and black. There was no wind and the night was freezing cold.

We were going through Witch's Waste for the second time. I was leading with Tulsi some twenty paces behind me. As usual, before going up to the field, I switched off the light and we stopped to listen. There seemed to be nothing near us and we could hear no pigs on the field ahead. We started forward again, but after I had gone only a short distance I stopped.

Tulsi was no longer behind me. I had missed his footsteps some time before, but thinking that he would soon catch up, I went on. Now a wave of annoyance passed through me: I could hear him down the path picking fruit—a thing he often did. I was about to call out to him when another sound stopped me. Something was moving on the path ahead, and it was moving boldly towards me. . .

Before going on I had better explain what the true position was at that moment. Tulsi had not stopped to pick fruit, but was standing still as a statue on the path forty yards behind me. For soon after I had switched off the torch and we started to move towards the field, he had seen a black shadow to the left of the path suddenly lope forward, stop at a bush, and then reach up to shake off the fruit. He stopped dead. He knew all about bears, and he knew that to call out might bring the unsuspecting animal straight at him; a moment later he saw me disappear round a bend in the path.

A few yards past this bend, I stopped when I missed him behind me. Almost at once I heard the noise on the path ahead. Although we were not to know it for a few moments more, we were in the middle of a family of three bears. Tulsi's eyes were riveted on the female, and coming down the path towards me, but still invisible, was a large male. Somewhere to the right of the path was a biggish cub, but neither of us yet knew anything about it.

The stage was now set for one of the biggest bits of confusion I've ever been mixed up in; and it came about because none of the actors in the play had the slightest idea of what was really happening. I, for my part, thought Tulsi was picking fruit and was quite unaware of the she-bear behind me. Tulsi could see her; but he had heard me stop, and he had also heard the other bear coming down the path ahead of me. But he didn't know that this was a bear. He thought it was me coming back to deal with *his* bear which he was quite sure I now knew about. On the top of all that muddle, none of the bears had the faintest notion that we were in their midst; for although they must have heard us, each of them must have assumed that we were some other member of their family moving about. . .

Believing that Tulsi was safe behind, I waited until the noise ahead of me materialized into a big black blob on the path. By then the rifle was already up to my shoulder and I switched on the torch. The beam showed a bear sitting up on its haunches like a huge black dog. The snowy-white U on its chest was brilliant in the light. I flicked the foresight on it and pressed the trigger. Without a sound the bear bounded off the path and disappeared into the undergrowth.

As the sound of the shot died away, a great bellowing bark of alarm shattered the night from somewhere close behind me. That was the first I knew of another bear and I spun round; but the curve of the path and a sprinkling of bushes prevented me seeing what was happening. But that a great deal was happening I couldn't doubt; for even before I had turned round the bear bellowed again and I heard it tearing through the undergrowth. Then something else started to run too just as another bear gave tongue from the other side of the path. Pandemonium came a second later. Bears in hysterics seemed to be crashing about all round me—and above the din was Tulsi's voice yelling for help. . .

What happened in those first few moments I pieced together from what I heard and from what Tulsi told me later. At the sound of the shot the she-bear whipped round as though she had been hit herself—and this is what Tulsi thought had happened. However, with her indifferent eyesight it is pretty certain that she still did not notice him standing a few yards away. Her first thought would have been for her cub somewhere on the other side of the path. Her bellow of alarm was to let the cub know where she was. Then she bounded off to meet it.

When Tulsi saw her lunge forward there was no doubt in his mind that he was being charged by a wounded bear. He started to run—and met the cub racing towards its mother. He ran slap into it and they crashed to the ground in each other's arms. A moment later Tulsi had rolled clear; but the cub had had the fright of its life and was now screaming its head off—and only a few yards away Mother was pounding up to the rescue.

No one will ever know whether she was bent on tearing Tulsi to pieces or whether she was so frightened herself that she was simply racing round in panic. But to both Tulsi and me it certainly seemed that she was out for blood. . .

For several seconds after the she-bear moved, I stood rooted to the spot. The sudden din from the bears and Tulsi was appalling and shifting so quickly that I was not sure which way to run. Then I raced down the path sweeping the light towards the side the din was coming from. All at once I saw the cub. Then Tulsi sprinted out from behind a bush. Right behind him was a bear. A moment later they had disappeared from sight behind another patch of cover. Now I could only hear them. All I could see was the tops of the bushes waving wildly as they crashed through.

Then I was bellowing to Tulsi to head for the light and warning him of the wounded bear somewhere ahead which may or may not have been dead. 'This way! This way!' I yelled. 'I can't shoot until I know where you are!'

The crashing through the bushes went on and I heard him shout something back. I was still yelling myself hoarse when he suddenly burst on to the path some yards to the left and came running towards me.

As he panted up, I heard the bear going across our front. I swung the light round and a moment later she was in the beam. Almost at the same time I saw the cub spring up from the undergrowth in front of her. They met with a bump and crashed down together; the next second they seemed to be fighting furiously as bears often do when they are frightened. I was sorry I had to kill the cub; but the bullet that finished his mother also broke his right front leg.

In the sudden silence that followed the two shots, Tulsi

and I said nothing. He was still out of breath and I could think of nothing to say. I fished out cigarettes and we sat on the path to smoke them. Then, in the distance, we heard the sound of shouting voices. At first we could not understand it; then we realized that the noise of the fracas had travelled three-quarters of a mile and woken everybody up at home. Even at that distance the noise had been so frightening that a rescue party was already on the way; it was coming in two bullock carts to carry back whatever was left of us. . .

That was the last time I went through Witch's Waste after dark while the ber fruit was on the bushes. The next night, on my own once more, I crossed it off my route and the field at the end of it was abandoned to the pigs. Eight good acres of nearly ripe peanuts—up till then comparatively little damaged.

TIGER IN A TYPHOON

It was 1955 and the hot weather nearly at an end. That year the heat had been appalling, and now, at the end of June, Babs and I were feeling the effects and scanning the skies each day for signs of rain. Around the estate everything was tinder-dry, and with the earth in the fields like lumps of iron it was difficult to get on with preparations for sowing. The rains were overdue, but the papers had at last told us that the monsoon had broken over southern India. All being well it should reach us within a few days.

Now that the rains were so close, it was time to inspect the nullahs and ravines which drain water from the land and lead it down to the Denwa River. At the start of the rains these often get clogged with fallen trees and the accumulated debris of the year. If this debris is allowed to collect trouble can follow: loose dams form quickly and then the force of the current soon jams everything into a solid and hard-to-move mass. That can mean flooded fields for perhaps the whole of the rains.

Another thing to watch for is the poachers' fish-traps which always appear just before the rains start. These are low, semi-circular walls of loose stone built across the nullahs with a small opening to channel the fish. Dams in miniature; but small as they are they soon collect debris and often cause a great deal of flooding if they are not found and demolished before the first waters swirl down to the river. One of the poachers' favourite spots, and also one where many natural dams build up, is the big nullah.

This is always the first place I go to when inspecting before the rains. Sure enough there was a half-completed fish-trap before I had gone a quarter of a mile. No one was near it when I came up, but farther along and round a bend I could hear voices and the sounds of men collecting stones from the nullah bed. I climbed the bank and waited behind a tree. There were two of them, and I let them get right back with their loads before I pounced. They were very sheepish and apologetic—as indeed they should have been; this nonsense has always been a sort of annual fixture and with monotonous regularity I catch the same men year after year. While they were knocking the wall down, I told them that they could rebuild it after the debris in the nullah had been swept away. They had known to start with that this permission was theirs simply by coming to ask for it; but as it is much easier to build a wall on dry sand than when water is racing down the nullah, the 'catch-me-if-you-can' tactics are always well worth trying.

When the last stone had been thrown down, Matchu, the elder of the two men, said: 'You want to see the tiger's kill?'

To hear him mention that again surprised me. While the wall was still standing, and while pleas were still being made for it to remain so, there had been a casual reference to a tiger's kill which they said they had found on their way to the nullah. The sudden introduction of that into the middle of the pleading had sounded so fishy that I took no notice; red herring of the same sort had been drawn across my path before. And not always without success, for on two occasions I had set off at once to investigate news of a very similar kind. In the heat of the moment the fish-traps had been forgotten; then—hours later—when nothing had been found and it seemed likely that I had been chasing a wild goose, I hadn't had the heart to send the culprits back to demolish their wall as I could not be sure I'd been had for a mug and that the poachers were not after all honest fellows only trying to be helpful.

'Where is the kill?' I asked. I was interested now and ready to believe that there might be something in the story. With the fish-trap down, they had nothing to gain by sending me off on a false scent.

Matchu pointed along the nullah: 'It's not very far down there, up on the left bank.' Then he added; 'We think it might be the Mograwallah.'

That was interesting indeed. The Mograwallah was a well-known cattle-thief which had been proscribed for more than a year. I motioned them to go ahead and we set off down the nullah. After following it for some three hundred yards, we climbed up the bank and then struck off through ground thickly covered with withered bushes and small trees. A short walk brought us up to a patch of thick jungle. Matchu pointed towards it with a finger to his lips. We went in quietly and after twenty yards, Matchu pointed again. The kill was a cow which had been dragged half under a spread of lantana and a heavy meal had been eaten off the hind-quarters. I was glad to see that it was not one of ours.

From where we were standing it was not far to the pool in the nullah, at this time of the year the only water for a long way around. When I had thanked the men for showing me the kill, I sent them away and then set off to the pool to see what I could find. The tiger's pug marks were all round the water.

Some of them were fresh, but a lot more showed that the tiger had been using the pool for perhaps two weeks; from the signs he was a nice animal and might well be the Mograwallah.

I had not been to the pool for quite a while, but two weeks is a longish time for a tiger to hang about and I was wondering why I had not heard of him. Half an hour later, I had found two more kills in that same patch of jungle. These were older than the first one, and both had been finished by hyenas which had scattered bones over a wide area. Like a lot of other cattle-killers, it looked as though the Mograwallah never returned to a kill after the first feed.

The three dead cows so close together and near the pool suggested that this tiger was unlikely to leave until after the rains had broken. He was obviously getting all he wanted to eat, and he was getting it from the hundreds of straying cattle now wandering the estate. During the hot months of the year these cattle are a perpetual nuisance; and for several reasons, all of them wrapped up in the Indian attitude towards cows, little or nothing can be done to keep them off the land.

The nuisance is considerable and begins each year as soon as the crops are cut. By this time the weather is warming up and the village pastures are already heavily over-grazed, so what the cattle owners do is drive their animals right out to fend for themselves. No one is in charge of them and they wander where they will; as the hot weather advances and the grazing grows even scarcer, the cattle have to keep feeding both by day and night just to stay alive. Until the rains revive the grass, none of them ever goes home for the good reason that there is nothing to eat there at all.

Sooner or later all these cattle wander to the estate where they try to stay. Along the river banks the pastures are naturally good and not overgrazed if we can stop it. But what a job trying to keep these strays away! The local cattle pound holds only forty animals and we have to deal with hundreds a day; but even if the pound held them all it would still be no solution. The cattle owners keep a wary eye cocked for anyone leading their animals to the pound; whenever our men appear with a bunch of strays word spreads rapidly and there is likely to be a fight. To this state of affairs officialdom merely shrugs its shoulders: the problems posed by Indian cows are so many that no one even tries to solve them. The only thing to do then is keep driving the strays away; but to employ men simply for this is not practical and so there are always scores of cattle wandering the estate.

A paradise for a cattle-killing tiger, and what this one was doing was simply staying put and picking off a cow whenever he was hungry. If he kept to the straying cattle I couldn't care less; but with our own herds wandering the estate too, and with small boys in charge of them, something would have to be done to end the Mograwallah's career.

Two days later, he killed again. The victim was another stray cow which he took at the top of the path coming up from the pool. Once more he had dragged the body into the same patch of jungle he had taken the others to. On the morning I found this kill, we'd had the first shower of the monsoon which had left the ground soft and the dry leaves sodden. The tiger had eaten a heavy meal and was not likely to be very far away. It was a good chance, for with the ground just right for stalking it might be possible to find him asleep.

It was another of those occasions when the tiger found me first and handed out a fright. It may be that I woke him suddenly or he might have been awake all the time and watching me from behind some bushes. Whatever the truth was, he gave no chance but sprang away with a roar when he decided that I was too close to be friendly.

On my way home for lunch, I saw that the black clouds were gathering again. At two o'clock the rain started, heavy stuff which left no doubt that the monsoon had at last arrived. To sit for a tiger in a deluge is neither sensible nor pleasant so I cancelled the machan I had told Bhutu to build. Besides, this tiger would now move off when the rain drove the straying cattle back to the shelter of their mangers.

The rain went on all night and there was no sign of it letting up by dawn the next morning. An hour later it was still very dark for the skies were a lowering mass of black, angry-looking clouds tinged with an ugly yellow. The rain started to come down harder and thunder began to growl overhead; by mid-morning the barometer on the veranda was as low as I had ever seen it.

The weather now looked ugly indeed and there was something about the sky that alarmed me; overhead the clouds seemed to be boiling as they lashed out the rain. A few seconds later I had forgotten them when, above the smashing of the deluge, I suddenly heard the roar of the rising river four hundred yards away. It was a sound that sent me hurrying back to my raincoat and gumboots.

The river of course always rises when the rains start and it often rises fast. But this rise was too sudden and suggested abnormal conditions which had not been there when I visited the river bank fifteen minutes before.

When I reached the river the roar of the racing waters was deafening. Far upstream I could see nothing of the causeway that takes the main road across the river-bed; in its place was a frothing, muddy-white line stretching from bank to bank. That meant a rise of nearly twenty feet in perhaps as many minutes: somewhere up in the mountains about Pachmarhi where the Denwa has its source, there must have been a lot more rain than even we'd had. After watching the river for some minutes I squelched across to the big nullah.

I found the water here already over the banks and flooding the land on both sides; the current down the centre was like a raging millstream. From force of habit, I started to splash through the water as near to the bank as I could judge. I was looking for the obstruction until I realized that there probably was none; the nullah just wasn't big enough to carry away the tons of water falling from the skies.

At three o'clock in the afternoon it was nearly dark and a high wind was rising steadily. The cattle, which had gone out as usual in the morning, had been brought back at midday and put in their shed. After that I had sent all the men back to their quarters; in this weather there was nothing anyone could do outside, and by the signs in the sky we had not yet seen the worst of it. The skies were getting darker, and as the rain pelted down the wind was rising to a high wailing shriek.

The typhoon struck soon after six. There was little warning, though a fiery blast of shattering thunder may have been its herald. A few seconds later, the elements went mad and the world was suddenly a howling inferno struck through with violent flashes of vivid violet light. The fury of the wind was frightening. It was roaring through the trees with a speed that appalled and the whole house was shuddering to the screaming impact. Above the deafening roar we could hear loud *snaps!* as branches were torn from the trees and the grinding crashes as forest giants slammed down before the onslaught.

Within fifteen minutes of the first blast, the roof of the cowshed was torn off bodily. We heard it start to tear loose, then came the rumble and rattle of falling bricks. Hard behind that rose the frantic cries of terrified cattle and the clatter of stampeding hooves on concrete. All at once the clatter stopped, bitten off by the wind with alarming suddenness.

As I looked at the damage the torch was hardly needed. The wreckage was brilliant under the almost continuous lightning. The roof had reared upwards and then levered down one entire longitudinal wall. The debris had fallen on the cattle and three of them were still writhing under a mass of splintered rafters and rubble; of the others there was no sign.

With four men carrying lanterns, I set off to look for them. The force of the wind now was such that the driving rain really hurt our bare hands and faces. We had scarcely gone two hundred yards to the north of the house when we were pulled up short. Stretching away into the night was a solid sheet of water. It covered the field in front of us to disappear into the trees fringing the far side; as far as we could see to the right and left of us there was water everywhere flooding up from the nullah.

We turned left and skirted along by the water. Almost at once we found the cattle. They had not gone far and were huddled together under some trees with the water lapping their legs. By now they had calmed down and gave no trouble when the men started to drive them home.

I left the men to it and then set off to find out how bad things really were. The rain was still slashing down, but even so the extent of the flooding from the nullah had come as a shock to me. What about the river? That was a much more formidable force and as I hurried across to it the first tinge of anxiety rose about the safety of the house.

The house is on a part of the estate which is roughly triangular. One side of the triangle is formed by the river. The other side is the nullah which, after running diagonally across the estate, meets the river to form the apex; about the centre of the base, between the river and the nullah, the house stands on a slight rise.

With my head down I turned into the wind and fought towards the river in a straight line. Even today I can recall vividly almost every step of that journey. It was like a waking nightmare with the wind nearly strong enough to lean on as it tore past with its unearthly shriek. Long before I should have reached the river my way was barred by its flooding waters coming to meet me. This was far worse than the nullah; you could see the water creeping up to the thunderous roar coming from behind the line of trees that marked the river bank in the rain-obscured distance.

I was just starting to move on to where the river meets the nullah, three-quarters of a mile from where I was standing, when I caught a sudden flurry of movement across the water in front of me. I switched on the torch quickly. Through the silvery rods of the rain smashing through the beam I saw a pack of wild dogs scampering towards me. They came on and then jumped to the dry land. They were within a few yards and all round me, whimpering and uttering sharp little cries of alarm; for all the notice they took of me I might not have been there.

As I walked on, I kept the light sweeping across the waters. After a few minutes I switched it off; the lightning was better, the almost continuous flashes lit the scene around me like daylight.

Not far on from where I had left the wild dogs I saw a small herd of spotted deer, four hinds and a stag, splashing out from a wood which in normal times is a hundred yards from the river; now it was an island of trees. They must have seen me as clearly as I could see them, but they splashed on, away from the greater danger of the rising water. When they had passed only a little way behind me, I went on. There was still no sign of the storm abating and the wind was driving the pelting rain as strongly as ever; the thunder was still crashing with scarcely a break. After another fifty yards, I stopped again.

This time there was no going on. The waters now were not only on my left but on my right as well, and just in front of me they met. The river and the nullah were now a single sheet of water. For a few moments I just stood still staring at the floods. The danger to the house now was very real. From where I was it was only a quarter of a mile away and the water were creeping towards it from two sides.

I turned quickly and started back. Almost at once I found myself in another nightmare of a different kind. Across my path there was suddenly a great sounder of pig standing motionless. To get past them I had to skirt to one side in spite of a great throat-tearing shout to move them. Then animals were everywhere. In the flashes from the skies I could see them all around me, some standing still while others moved slowly as though in a dream. I did not know then that we were all on an island only some ten acres in extent which was rapidly growing smaller.

When I got back to the house, Babs had some coffee waiting on the stove. When I had gulped it down I went out again to see the cattle. They had been put in an old and long-disused 'country' shed. The roof was of rough thatch, the sides built of light stakes lashed together with strips of bamboo; the only reason why this was still standing was probably because the wind had no 'push' against its openwork sides.

The cattle were very restless. Now that they were locked up again the collapse of the roof in their old shed was obviously still a vivid memory. They were milling around wildly, barging into one another and crashing against the flimsy sides. If this shed collapsed it would not be the wind but the cattle which pulled it down. But there was nowhere else to put them, the three other sheds were some distance from the house and were already under water when I passed them on my way back.

Half an hour later, I went out again. The swollen nullah was now within a hundred yards of the house and the river had swept across the base of the triangle to join it. The area of our island had now shrunk to about three acres—and there was still no sign of the rain stopping.

On my way back to the house, I had another look at the cattle. They were still very restless but still safe inside. That hardly seemed to matter now. I was going to give the rain another hour and if it had not stopped then I should let them out to take their chance in the floods.

Some twenty minutes later, as we were sitting in a room at the back of the house, it seemed to me that the rain had suddenly slackened. I got up and went out towards the front veranda. When I reached the door leading to it I stopped and looked out. There was no light outside and none in the room behind me. Beyond the veranda the lightning was vivid, the scene beneath it as light as day. The rain *was* stopping. Then, as I stared out at it, a slight movement from the left turned my eyes.

A tiger was standing at the end of the veranda. It had been the merest flash of a picture but clear beyond mistake. The lightning flashed again and it was still there.

A moment later I was in the back room grabbing for the rifle. The magazine was full and a torch mounted on the barrel for I had only recently put it down. Back again at the veranda door, I peered round. The tiger was still there and I snapped on the light. But he didn't wait a second. As the light hit him he sprang . . . out of it and away into the night. The bullet I sent after him was wide and smacked into a concrete trough in the garden.

It was the last straw for the cattle. In his flight the tiger streaked past their shed. That was all they needed: a strong whiff of tiger slammed into their nostrils by the wind. They were stampeding wildly before the echoes of the shot died away. There was a violent crash and the shed was match-wood. Then the cattle were out and thundering away snorting with terror.

As the sounds of their flight faded I suddenly realized that the rain had stopped. All at once the main sound of the night was the mighty roar of the river. A good sound now. One that told that the dangers of the floods were over. The river falls just as fast as it rises and that loud booming proclaimed that the waters were receding and racing away to the sear.

What the extent of the damage was I could not even guess, but that was something to worry about in the morning. In the meantime we had to round up the cattle again and somehow bed them down for the rest of the night. That should not take long: they could not have gone far as they would certainly keep to the dry land about the house. That there was also a tiger somewhere in that small area was not really much to worry about. That beast had plenty of troubles of his own, for if ever I had seen a frightened animal it was this tiger when he sprang away from the veranda. For him it had been any port in the worst storm of his life, and he had been on the veranda only because it must have seemed to him the one safe spot in a world suddenly gone mad.

Nor did he in fact give any trouble. The cattle were rounded up safely and left in an open compound at the back of the house. By breakfast time the next morning, the river was nearly back in its bed and the sun was shining brightly from a blue sky. When the cattle went out to graze I told the boys in charge of them not to go too far from the house. After such an exciting night that tiger might be hungry. . .

EPILOGUE

Has it all been worth it? And do we ever regret choosing to live in a lonely place like this?

As I write these words more than ten years have passed and that is time enough to have made up our minds one way or the other. The truth is that we would not change this life for any other, and it would also be true to say that we hardly miss the old kind of life at all. This quite frankly surprises us whenever we think about it. Before the war one of my dearest possessions was a 'blown Merc' and I never thought life could be complete without theatres and cinemas and the cheerful chatter of a village pub. Perhaps it was the knock on the head or perhaps the first signs of old age that brought about the change; for certain it is now that I miss none of the things I used to imagine made life worth living. Today, a leisurely bullock-cart is all I ask for to get about in.

Babs feels much the same. With all the animals she can keep now and a host of other interests she is never bored. Even so, we do occasionally wonder why we miss the old life and all the amusements that went with it so little. We are still not sure of the real reason, but whenever we look back to life as it was before, the picture nearly always is a blur of movement as it shows a frantic rush from one pursuit to another. Our lives were ruled by engagement books and 'dates' and the ringing of the phone; in some way we were always bound to others with invisible chains of 'arrangements'. Here, in the old sense of the word, there are no others to make arrangements with, and there are certainly no amusements to keep us up half the night. It is of course a matter of temperament, and you either like this sort of life or you hate it, because there is no halfway. To us, however, the feeling of untrammelled freedom compensates for everything. On top of that life is uncomplicated and there is time to relax—something we were never able to do properly before.

We remember, too, how often those old amusements palled. One party was much like another, and at the end of any show—no matter how good it had been or on what medium—there was always a vague sense of anticlimax when the lights went up. As you rubbed your eyes it came to you that nothing of what you had just seen had been real; it had all been some momentary magic which had whisked you off to an exciting world and then dropped you back with a sudden bump to a tame one. But it was magic that served a purpose, and the time, which might otherwise have been a bore, had passed pleasantly. I believe the truth was that we were satiated with too many amusements which came too near to perfection. Nothing was really new any more. With coloured talkies and television wonders had ceased, and until some fresh and staggering invention arrived to revive our interest again, we were only lukewarm and getting more and more difficult to please.

Many of our old friends have admitted that since the war they have found it hard to settle down to the old routine and that there are often times when they are bored to tears.

This, I think, would eventually have happened to me.

That it hasn't and that I'm never bored is almost certainly because anything that happens here is real and life is often full of surprises; it's the difference between finding a tiger at the bottom of the garden and the fairies.

And the Congress government? Is it as anti-British as we were led to believe? Have we, in fact, been singled out and unfairly treated in any way?

Quite the reverse has been the truth, and there are several ministers and executives of our State Government who have deliberately gone far out of their way to help us many times. This help has taken many forms, and it would be right to say that no reasonable request we have ever made has been turned down. No, by and large, Indians are one of the friendliest of peoples and few of them indeed still harbour any resentment against the British.

That last paragraph may leave the impression that life at Mandikhera has always gone like a song and that we have never had any troubles. In actual fact, however, we have had more than our fair share of troubles and not a few very real alarums and excursions quite unconnected with tigers. One day I may write another book about the stirring times that followed the finding of gold and diamonds on the estate. I say 'may write' because my old idea that a writer's life was one of idleness and ease was rudely shattered the moment I took up my pen. Of all the forms of self-torture this is the most exquisite—and that was something I found out just when I'd decided that the one-day week was not so impossible after all.

Yes, the really simple life in a place miles from anywhere can boil down to a lot of leisure you never had before. It's not everybody's cup of tea, but we have never had a single regret and should certainly miss it if we ever had to change.

ACKNOWLEDGEMENTS

Before starting this book I should like to put on record my sincerest thanks to the editor of *Blackwood's Magazine* who published the first story I wrote. This was *The Langra Tigress*, the first part of which appears here as 'The Odd Chance'. That first acceptance encouraged me to write more stories which in time came into the pages of *Maga* and are now in this book: 'Eight Annas a Tail', 'Joe', 'Never Be Too Sure', 'Midnight Encounter', 'Tiger in a Typhoon'.

I am also grateful to the editor of *Wide World* who printed a story called 'The Mowha Maneater', some of which is in 'The Three Bears'.

My special thanks are also due to the editor of the American magazine *True*, who gave me my first chance in the States when he published 'Tigers' Trap' and 'Never Be Too Sure' under the title of *Cat and Man Game.*

Printed in Dunstable, United Kingdom

67813800R00133